SWAN SONG

SWAN SONG

ISABEL BERCAW

Copyright © 2024
GRAE Entertainment
All rights reserved.

This is a work of fiction. Unless otherwise indicated, all the names, characters, businesses, places, events and incidents in this book are either the product of the author's imagination or used in a fictitious manner. Any resemblance to actual persons, living or dead, or actual events is purely coincidental.

Content Warning:
This book contains discussions of and depictions of mental health-related topics and is intended for adult readers. If you or someone you know is struggling, there are ways to get help. Text HOME to 741741 to connect with a volunteer Crisis Counselor or call the 24 hour National Suicide Prevention Lifeline at 1-800-273-8255. The purpose of this novel is not to diagnose, treat, or provide medical or mental health advice in any way.

DEDICATION

To anyone who's ever lost hope.

Part 1

PREFACE

*T*he glowing logs in the fireplace sputter and pop in a labored search for their final breaths. The room is thick with darkness, but I feel safe sitting at the foot of his navy velvet armchair. In one hand, he holds an empty crystal glass, and with the other, he twirls my fine locks in his fingers as I scan the pages of the book sitting in the lap of my lilac-colored dress. My hands and arms are spotless and fair. My cheeks toast in the fire's warmth. "She's so beautiful," he whispers to no one, with whiskey breath. Cigar smoke drifts off a side table and dances in the air, *teasing my eyes and nose with a funny hot itch. I welcome it. I breathe in what he's blown out. As I exhale, he suddenly latches onto a whole handful of my hair, interrupting the pattern of docile twirling he had been so gently executing before. It catches me off guard. I don't have time to run or call out for help. He lurches forward and pulls my head close to his face so that his nose is pressed into my forehead. His grasp is so tight his fist shakes. "Why are you so beautiful?" he seethes, quietly but passionately, with a sharp rain of saliva that sprays onto my toasty cheek. The words sizzle in my ear. Without moving my head from his face, he slams the glass he'd been holding into the walnut floor, and with the shatter, I scream, breaking my silence. He rises from the chair, my hair still locked in his hand, and before I can resist, he heaves me into the glass shards. I whimper in fear. He grabs his cigar from the side table, discards a clump of mousy hair onto the floor, and sucks a final puff of smoke from the stogie as he does so. I watch the hair as it floats to his feet. He walks toward me, takes a knee, and puts his grounded foot heavy on my ankle. I begin to pant and flail in a panic, but he slams my chest down with his free arm, and my back is beat into a salty crust of glass. He presses the smoking tip of his cigar into the top of my calf. I wail as it eats through my delicate skin, like spit eroding cotton candy.*

1.

I shoot up in bed with a gasp. After a moment, I pull my bony knees to my chest and catalog reality. Soft sunlight has just begun to peek through my window, over a row of plants, and into my Boston apartment. The beams dot my white wall with a pattern of golden freckles. They dust my short dresser and tall bookshelf and refract in my fishbowl. My fish, Fish, must feel like he's at a rave or perhaps laser tag. Thinking about a goldfish playing laser tag encourages me to grin. Slowly, the feelings invoked by my dream dissolve. Unbothered by the cold pool of sweat I'm huddled in, I move my hand to rest a pair of fingers on the thick button of scar tissue on the back of my leg. I breathe in deeply, breathe out, and hoist myself out of my sticky sheets with a little hop.

The dark wooden floor creaks as I make my way to my bathroom. I brush my teeth and comb my short auburn-brown hair. Then I wash my face and smear on some minimal makeup that's probably all the wrong shades for my pale complexion and hazel-green eyes. I slap on a shirt, plop a few food pellets into Fish's tank, wash my pill down with black coffee, and stuff my backpack with the books I'll need for today's classes. Then, I sling on my backpack after my jacket and hustle downstairs and out into the frosty streets of Cambridge.

The winter air is hard on my lungs. I'm not wearing a scarf or a hat and the cold turns the peaks of my cheeks and the tip of my nose into summits of frosty mountains. The useless November sun has risen only in brightness and aches in my eyes. I squint my way through the walk to campus.

After entering the building I'm due in, I start to thaw. The heat is always blasting in my classroom, roasting the students like marshmallows. I take my usual seat in the back and wait for my professor to come in. I'm technically three minutes late, but luckily, Professor Bowling is always five minutes late, so I'm actually two minutes early. After two semesters of class with him, he's become rather predictable. Right on cue, at 10:05 AM, Professor Bowling casually enters the classroom, grinning as if he did us all a favor by being tardy. But his generosity lives in vain. Usually, several master's students who still don't know how to manage their time roll in for another few minutes post-Bowling's arrival, so he takes his time getting situated. He removes a black fedora hat from his smooth head and sets it neatly on his desk. He then takes off his thick beige trench coat with a *whoosh*, unveiling one hell of an outfit. Today, Bowling is wearing a brown tweed suit set, with a pink bow tie and dress shoes. He wears an outfit equally as extravagant to every class, and I'd be lying if I said I didn't look forward to his bi-weekly fashion spectacle. However, his coordination skills seem to never be fully utilized when dressing himself. He must be either colorblind or careless in this department. Or, more likely, he dreadfully pairs his clothes together on purpose. No matter; it only contributes to my fondness for him. He's quite an eccentric man in the areas I've witnessed and is seldom careless in any department as far as I can tell. He's certainly not careless in the literature department. He's one of the most intelligent people I've met. Sometimes, if I read what he tells me to read and think about what he tells me to think about, it almost inspires me to write.

"Good morning, *Dead Poets Society*!" he says enthusiastically, referring to what he's named the class. He must be quite proud of it, as he mentions it at every possible chance he gets. "How is everyone doing this morning?"

His voice is smooth and bold like a nice espresso. Two of the twelve kids in the room respond with a halfhearted *good*. I'm not one of them, but still, I'm mad at everyone else for not responding. I guess, like myself, many of these students chose to get an MFA not purely out of passion for the craft of literature, but to also stall entering the real world. No matter; I want Professor Bowling to feel validated standing in front of our lazy, sleep-deprived class in his crisp ensemble. I look up to him with empathy at his podium. He carries on, unbothered.

"Today we are going to begin the process of extrapolating meaning in the works of one Sylvia Plath in relation to relevant themes in this class."

There was certainly a much more efficient way to explain we were starting a new unit on a dead poet but I can't bring myself to be annoyed. I rest my head on my hand and instinctively begin to twirl a lock of hair behind my ear.

"Ladies and Gentlemen, let's start with a tidbit of history, shall we?"

Sometimes I can't tell if Professor Bowling lived in England for a stretch of time or just talks in a dialect as old as he looks. Whatever the case, his linguistics are on brand.

"Sylvia Plath was born in Boston in 1932 and infamously took her own life in her London home when she was thirty years of age."

A stiffening takes place in my neck and shoulders. I continue twirling my hair.

"During her tragically short life, however, Ms. Plath produced an astonishing amount of content, with her most famous work likely being her novel *The Bell Jar*, which you will begin reading for homework. Today, however," Bowling announces, with a small grimace, as he reaches for the projector screen's handle, "we will 'ease' into her works, if you will, with… this!" he exclaims as he theatrically lowers the projector screen. It retracts with a screech into a compact cocoon near the ceiling in a bold act of basic physics.

He looks at us expectantly, almost as if waiting for applause. No one moves, except for one student who'd fallen asleep and been reawakened at the screen's commotion.

This underwhelming group response makes me blush with second-hand embarrassment; however, Bowling's own first-hand embarrassment is either not present or concealed impossibly well. I suppose, to leave your house wearing clothing like he does, you must be pretty damn sure of yourself. I grin at him from the back of the class in a small showcase of appreciation, then direct my attention to the chalkboard, where there is a poem written out in perfect cursive letters, which reads:

> *Herr God, Herr Lucifer*
> *Beware*
> *Beware.*
> *Out of the ash.*
> *I rise with my red hair*
> *And I eat men like air.*

"What do you all observe here, anything?" Bowling asks. There is a long pause. And a dire lack of enthusiasm in this class. Finally, a girl in a yellow sweater and loafers in the front raises her hand. I keep my own hand behind my ear, twirling, and now, gently tugging on my hair.

"Yes, thank you, Ms. Druckman," Bowling says, motioning to a girl named Abigail, whose arm sits half-outstretched into the air.

"Well, the imagery of the poem really reminds me of a phoenix rising from the ashes, the ashes being a sort of purgatory between heaven and hell, as indicated by the God and Lucifer reference in the beginning line," Abigail says.

"Yes, brilliant!" Bowling beams, like she's just offered him a free annual subscription to the bowtie-of-the-month club. "And notice the genius in the word choice," Bowling adds. "Plath never actually says 'between heaven and hell' or explicitly states it's a phoenix rising from the ashes of ill fate, yet you were still able to see exactly what Plath wanted you to. Many poets are able to rhyme, connect themes, and tell stories, but what makes some poetry exceptional is its ability to show the readers something without explicitly telling them what they want them to see. They make metaphors within metaphors. This is a trademark of Plath's craft and an excellent example of her vast capabilities in manipulating the English written language, which we will see later that she does so in a prose-like fashion when writing fiction."

Bowling's passion must have sparked something because the guy who'd been sleeping earlier flings up a letter-jacketed arm.

"Yes, Matt," Bowling says, failing to hide his surprise at Matt's willing participation.

"What's that last part, there, about… man-eating?" Matt asks.

"Well, what do *you* think it's about?" Bowling refutes warmly.

"Ummm, maybe like… feminism?" Matt says, with a subtle undertone of concern. If his football friends were here, they'd probably laugh at this for reasons they don't fully understand.

"Well, there certainly is a feminist tone here, consistent with Plath's groundbreaking views for her time, but it's a bit more complicated than that. This question is a good one, and actually leads me to the first theme I'd like to point out in Plath's writing, which is one of isolation in individuality in juxtaposition with a strong yearning for independence."

A girl blurts out, "Okay, so Plath wanted a little agency and people decided this was feminist, which made her lonely."

Bowling nods with an encouraging smile, then carries on with his point.

"Exactly. You see, Plath lost her father at a very young age, eight years old to be exact. This traumatic event would become a huge factor in her writing. In fact, in almost all of her work, her father is mentioned at least once, if not marked as the main subject of the piece."

The classroom suddenly feels warmer than usual. A soft buzz grows behind my ear. I build the intensity at which I'm pulling on the lock. I feel my heartbeat in my fingertips as my hand coaxes the hair from my scalp. A single strand detaches from my head with a slippery *pop*.

"Sylvia absolutely idolized her father, Otto, all while harboring a slight guilty resentment for his departure. Otto Plath was also a writer and highly educated, which inspired Sylvia's dedication to her own education. It is said that after he died, she kept

Otto's personal dictionary and would obsessively comb through each page, circling the words she found significant."

An urgent emptiness wells inside of me. I beckon it from my skin and unearth it as I tug. *Pop. Pop. Pop.* The hairs are plucked off my head like flowers, followed by a prickling relief. But as the sensation fades and the relief with it, the emptiness clings to me like a weed. I keep pulling, hoping to get to the root of this feeling, but it's nowhere to be found. Still, I dig for it. I retreat into a sore rhythm. *Pop. Pop. Pop.*

"Sylvia's obsession with her departed father is certainly a significant source of her socially masculine tendencies for the time. As she became more obsessed with him, she became more like him. But where her obsession is most reflected isn't in her gendered habits. It's in the reflection of manic grief within her craft. She simply could not let go of her father's memory. It's what made her brilliant. And it's ultimately what destroyed her."

When the lecture is over, I step over a little bouquet of hair at the leg of my chair.

2.

Lillian Gasper and I have been getting coffee together every day for almost a year and a half, ever since we met at a first-year orientation event. Lillian is a hoot. Her mom is the CFO of Ralph Lauren, but her favorite thing in the world is thrift shopping—except for when she's buying jewelry. She wears shiny Cartier rings and Van Cleef and Arpels necklaces and Tiffany earrings. She has eight piercings; only six of them are visible through her ears. Her dad is also in finance, and her parents practically forced her to go to business school, where she sticks out like a sore thumb amongst the button-down clad Wall Street worshippers. She bleaches her hair bright-blonde and dyes the ends a different color every other month. She wears sharp navy blue eyeliner. She gets each nail painted a different color because she can't choose just one polish. She grew up on the Upper East Side and could've been a prima ballerina with NYC Ballet, but quit when the company wouldn't let her audition for Romeo in *Romeo and Juliet*. She brought her cat, named Bean, that she's allergic to, to Boston with her in a rented baby yellow Volkswagen Beetle because although she could afford to fly, she wanted Bean to be able to see the countryside for once. She's been a vegan just about every other week for the time that I've known her. Once she took a two-week vow of silence in the name of animal rights awareness and lasted thirty minutes.

I bite the inside of my lip on my way to The Coffee Shop. When I get there, Lillian's already waiting at our table with her usual order– an iced almond milk chai tea latte for sipping, and an extra hot whole milk cappuccino for dipping. She always has a croissant for breakfast and likes to dunk it in cappuccino foam, but she doesn't drink the cappuccino itself. It's incredibly wasteful, and quite entertaining. I walk across the small rustic café and up to the register and when I open my mouth to order, I taste iron.

"May I have a double shot of espresso, please?" I ask the barista with a smile. I haven't seen him here before. He has kind brown eyes. I empathize with baristas, especially the ones that have to deal with Lillian.

"Sure, no milk or anything, just espresso?" he confirms, in some kind of British accent.

"No, thank you; espresso is perfect," I reply, enjoying the oddity of his accent in my ears.

"Sweet, for here or to go?" he asks.

"For here, please."

"Okay, $4.25 please. And can I get a name for the order?" he asks.

"Julia. Keep the change," I say, handing him a five-dollar bill.

"Thank you!"

I smile to myself and walk over to where Lillian is sitting in the corner. Today she's wearing a long black romper decorated with printed kiss marks in various shades of pink lipstick. It goes nicely with the pink ends of her hair.

"Hey babes," Lillian greets me with sunny suspicion, "are we going to address the Brit in the room?"

"The new barista?" I confirm.

"Duh! He's super hot!" she says in an urgent hush.

"Yeah, I guess." I agree.

"Oh, don't act like you didn't notice; there was no missing *that* bone structure!" she points out.

I steal a glance at him from across the room.

"Yeah, he's not bad," I say, prompting Lillian to roll her eyes at my reservation.

"How was your class?" she asks.

"It was good. How was your morning?" I ask, chewing on the inside of my cheeks like gum between sentences.

"It was pretty good, but when I got back after my first chai, Bean had eaten my entire basil plant and then threw up in my bed right before I had to leave."

"Ugh, ew, I'm sorry. Is he okay?" I ask. Lillian usually gets coffee three to four times a day.

"He's fine, just a pain in the ass," she criticizes.

"Julia!" a deep voice calls from the counter.

"One sec," I say to Lillian, and get up to grab my espresso.

Before, when I'd spoken to the barista, I'd been too focused on ordering nicely to notice just how handsome he was. But after this trip to the counter, I now understand what Lillian was talking about. He has overall strong, dark features with sharp accents, that is, with the exception of his lips. They look quite soft. I don't ruminate on it. I only blush, take my drink, and go back to my seat.

"Duuuude," Lillian says, wide-eyed and grinning, "He was totally checking you out."

"Who?" I act oblivious, attempting to conceal my interest for no good reason.

"The barista, of course. Who else?" She sees through me. "He was smiling at you so big I would've thought you asked him for a shot of espresso with a side of his dick in your mouth!"

I nearly spit out my mouthful of coffee as she says this. "Oh my god, he was probably just being friendly to make up for burning the shit out of the beans on his first day!"

"Sure, but it doesn't matter what kind of coffee he makes as long as he makes good love." She laughs, and I smile at her quick humor. As I take another piping hot sip, Lillian grimaces.

"Ugh, I never understand how you drink that shit," she says.

I shrug and put down the cup. Suddenly, Lillian looks concerned.

"Wait, Julia, I think you're bleeding on your lip." She points to her own pink lip.

I touch my hand to the corner of my mouth where she's pointing and when I pull it back, sure enough it's coated in red. "That's weird," I say and quickly wipe my mouth with the back of my hand.

Lillian looks at me very seriously and leans across the table.

"Is it?" she asks. "Have you been having nightmares again?"

"No, no, I'm good; I just must've bitten my tongue by accident."

"While you were chewing your espresso?"

I don't say anything.

Lillian's eyes narrow. "I knew it. When did they start back up?" she asks.

"A couple of weeks ago," I shrug defensively. "But it's okay; I'm fine."

"I thought they were getting better, you barely even had any last semester! Are you taking your meds?"

"I take them religiously, but even on medication, people have ups and downs. And like I said, I'm fine," I say flatly.

"You're not fine if these dreams are stressing you out so much that you start hurting yourself again–"

"It's not like that; I'm seriously okay. This is why I didn't tell you, because I didn't want you to worry," I affirm.

"Listen," Lillian says, "I'm not trying to make you feel bad or anything; I just think if you're having your nightmares again and your habits are coming back, it wouldn't be a bad idea to just, I don't know, maybe talk to your psychiatrist or someone about it? The worst that can happen is that nothing improves."

"Worst case scenario, they lock me up in an insane asylum because I have a couple bad habits and when I want to leave they say I'm nuts and sell my organs." I joke, wanting to stop talking about this.

"I thought you were studying poetry, not drama." She humors me. "Slow down with the theatrics. You're not going to get locked up because you go to therapy. I just think if you're hurting yourself, you should talk to a professional, because as much as I want to be able to help you, I can only do so much." She hesitates. "And with what happened, you know, to your dad…" She looks down, ashamed for me. "I just—I don't want to see you get hurt again, or worse." She concludes, taking my hand in her own from across the table.

"Okay, sure, I know. I'll think about it," I tell her, but the mere thought of mental hospitals makes me nauseous.

"Okay, thank you," she tells me, and we both take an uncomfortably long swig of coffee. "On a lighter note, what're you doing tonight? There's a swanky house party in Charlestown later at Jerrod's. Mr. and Mrs. Kaminski are out of town, and it's gonna be litty titty, so we should go." Jerrod is one of Lillian's boyfriends.

"What? Is he sixteen years old, having a party while his parents are away?" I ask, judgmental, but grateful for the subject change. Lillian is never one to dwell on a topic.

"I don't know; all I know is they have a really nice brownstone. He probably sees it as compensation for watering their plants or something. That's not the point. The point is free booze and something to do on a Friday night."

"Okay, maybe, what time?" I ask.

"It starts at nine. Come on, it'll be fun."

"Okay, fine." I agree.

The rest of the day passes slowly; it always does when I have plans at night. I don't have any more classes on Fridays, so I just study for a bit at The Coffee Shop and then, when Lillian has to leave, I migrate to the library to try and get some writing done. I pull out my notebook and start scribbling away, and when I'm finished, there is a dramatic little poem glaring back at me from the screen.

When the day is done and the sun has set
And you're taking in your final breath
And you can't find your heart, there's no beat in your chest
And it's never enough when you're trying your best

It's not finished, but I decide it's good enough for now, tear it from my notebook, and stow it away for a future workshop class. Then, I study my assigned readings for the weekend, except for *The Bell Jar*. This takes up most of my day. Around 6 PM, I take the long route back to my apartment, buy Lillian a new basil plant at my corner store, and head home. When I enter my unit, hunger braids my stomach. I decide I should probably eat something before the party so I can drink a little more. I scramble some eggs with cheese and douse them in hot sauce, and by the time I'm done with my dinner, it's time to start getting ready for the night.

"What d'ya think, Fish?" I ask as I hold up two different tops against my body in front of his tank. He squirms his little golden body back and forth across the face of the bowl. This was not very helpful, but I'm not sure what I was expecting when I asked a fish for fashion advice. I pick a maroon long-sleeve top that my stepsister gave me, then pull on a pair of black pants and slide on some black wedges, which will absolutely have my feet throbbing by the end of the night. Then, I *click-clack* my way to my bathroom and plug in my hair straightener so it can get hot while I layer some more makeup over whatever is left on my face from this morning. A little eyeliner and lipstick later, I don't look terrible, so I move onto my hair. I clamp the hot mouth of the iron around ribbons of hair and drag it down their entirety, making them feathery and soft. The motion is smoothly redundant.

As I work my way around my head with the device, my mind doddles its way back to the poem from Professor Bowling's lecture. *Out of the ash, I rise with my red hair.* I picture a silky plump Venus, naked, with long auburn curls, gracefully emerging from a blanket of chalky gray ash. Reborn from the fire that destroyed her. *And I eat men like air.* Our class got it wrong, I realize.

Plath wasn't wanting to eliminate men in some feminist plot. She was trying to take them in. To fill a void with them. A deep untouchable space for her father. A feeling of emptiness that no heaven can cure. One that no hell can replace– *Tsss!* I gasp and instinctually pull away as the heat of the iron kisses my neck. The concentrated bite brings my brain to a halt.

I slowly lower the device in my hand until it's level with the bathroom countertop, but I don't set it down. I stare at it deeply with a repulsive hunger. *Turn it off,* I tell myself. But I don't. I'm stuck in a standoff between what I want to want and what I really want. *Turn it off.* But I can't. The mouth of the device radiates a heated promise—that of a burn. This tugs at me like a magnet. I move the iron in my right hand to my left wrist and let it hover there, centimeters over my skin. I can feel the heat swelling, curling around my joint. My heartbeat pounds in my veins and drums in my ears. My stomach flutters. The hair on my arm stands up. I take a deep, slow breath, in and out. I move to clamp the iron down when the chime of my cell phone in my pocket breaks my concentration. In a jump, I toss the iron at the counter and then yank the cord from the outlet. When I pull out my phone, there's a text from Lillian letting me know she's waiting for me outside my building. I inhale, exhale, regain my bearings, then exit the bathroom.

"Bye, Fish!" I say, and grab my black trench coat from my closet and a small crossbody purse and head downstairs.

Lillian is still wearing her kiss-marked romper and she's added a brown faux fur coat and is carrying a banana-yellow handbag. She has on cat-eyed sunglasses with thick, shiny black rims, even though it's been dark for over two hours.

"Babes, you look so good, my sexy!" she flirts, moving the sunglasses up and down with her hand from the post behind her ear like an intrigued cartoon character.

"Thanks," I laugh, "did you pregame?" I can never tell if she's drunk or just being her wonderfully weird self.

"Hell yeah, I'm not walking half a mile in this weather without an alcohol blanket!" She says, giving me a fuzzy hug. She smells like a high quality stripper.

"Smart," I tell her as we begin to walk down the lamp post-lit cobblestone streets of Cambridge towards Jerrod's house.

"How was the rest of your day?" Lillian asks.

"Decent, you?" I reply.

"Same here—do you like my sunglasses?" she asks.

"I do."

"I bought them today, in between classes. They were on sale," she reveals, before promptly tripping over an unearthed sidewalk brick.

"Motherfucker, that hurt! I stubbed my toe!" she yells, stumbling to steady herself.

"Oh God, are you okay?" I ask with jealous compassion.

"Yeah, I'll live," she grumbles and moves the sunglasses to the top of her head, "Oh my god, I forgot to tell you," she says, grabbing my arm. "I ran into Henry today during my lunch, and he said he's coming to Jerrod's."

"Yeah, I figured he would be," I tell her, even though I hadn't even considered Henry's potential presence at the party prior to Lillian's news. The prospect of seeing him makes my insides quiver.

Henry Langmore is a ham of a man. Standing at over six feet tall and weighing in at over two hundred pounds, made purely of protein shakes and chicken, one might describe him as hot if it weren't for the light mullet and silly mustache he's recently started to push. If he'd grown up in Australia, he'd most certainly have played rugby, but he didn't. Instead, he grew up in Nebraska and plays the gym. He got his master's in exercise science or something last year but stayed in Boston after graduation. I'm fairly certain he uses self-tanner lotion. He might also use bleaching shampoo to keep his hair light, but I have yet to find that in any of his bathroom cabinets. We met on a dating app that Lillian made me download, and he and I hit it off. For the larger part of the past semester, we've been a subtle item, and that's just the way I like it. Henry never had any intention of actually dating me or anyone, and he made that quite clear from the start. I liked that he was straightforward. Online dating, I learned, can be a dreadful thing. It really is quite absurd what people will say to you behind a phone screen. Henry was no exception to this rule. And Henry delivers on his promises—that's the only thing I've told Lillian about what we do together.

"You're going to have a fun night," Lillian winks at me.

3.

Notes of shitty rap music and various flavors of vape pen smoke spill out of the cracked open windows of the brownstone, as Lillian and I arrive. Either Jerrod thinks he's a bigger deal than he is, or he's grasping at some ploy for responsibility because there are a couple of frat-looking boys playing secret service at the door. We walk past a few shadowy smokers and up some concrete steps to where they guard the entrance.

"First and last names," the shorter of the two boys requests with a comical degree of sincerity.

"Lillian Gasper and Julia Wright," Lillian says. He writes them down in the notes app of his phone.

"Are you two over twenty-one?" he asks and a breathy laugh escapes from my nose. Lillian elbows me, unfortunately not hard enough to do any damage.

"Yes, she's twenty-four, and I'm twenty-five," she says truthfully, jabbing a thumb in my direction. She looks up at them with fuck me eyes, playing along with their power trip.

"All right, go on in," the other one says. Once we're in, I turn to Lillian.

"What, are they expecting the president to show up and do keg stands with us?"

"I don't know," she laughs, "sometimes you just have to let guys like that have their moment. Plus, look around, this doesn't exactly give off a keg stand kind of vibe."

Lillian is right. Despite the tacky rap, the setting is oddly romantic. The lights are dimmed. There's a disco ball somewhere, spraying rainbow polka-dots across an antique runner-clad staircase. The guests are dressed somewhere between wanting to be classy and naked. Thongs peek out of pleated skirts. Pressed white shirts are unbuttoned and display trimmed chest hair. Glow sticks are layered between pearls and diamonds. Someone is pouring Veuve-Clicquot into a red plastic cup. Even the fruity nicotine vapor, accumulating in the air like fog, adds to the ambiance of it all.

"I smell private school," Lillian whispers, a bit too loudly, and leads the way through the sitting room to a makeshift bar table. Behind it sits Jerrod, with a red and green striped tie fashioned around his brown head of hair. His blue eyes are bloodshot and his white button down clings to his skinny body, damp with sweat.

When he sees us, he yells, "Lillyyyy!" with his arms outstretched, double-fisting a bottle of beer and a handle of Patron tequila.

"Jesus, Jerrod, it's not even ten yet, are you chasing tequila with beer already?" Lillian asks. Jerrod checks his silver Omega watch and smirks.

"Hell no, I'm chasing beer with tequila! Jules, how's it hanging?" he asks me, and then without pausing for me to respond, says, "Can I get you two anything to drink?"

"I don't know, if my ID is fake, are you gonna call your rent-a-bouncers to kick me out?" Lillian says with a big, sarcastic pout.

"Oh, yeah, the guys at the front, sorry about that. Don't mind them; that was just part of the 'rents deal," Jerrod says, abbreviating the word *parents* in a true asshole fashion.

"Deal?" Lillian asks.

"Yeah, like if I was going to throw a big party, I needed to find some kind of security, 'cause last time my sister threw one, a bunch of our doorknobs went missing," he explains.

"HA," Lillian laughs out loud, "Sorry about that; they were just so pocketable, I couldn't help myself!"

"Yeah, it was funny until we found out they were vintage or something and essentially irreplaceable—like one of a kind knobs," he grumbles.

Lillian reaches over the table and touches his arm. "Just like yours," she says with a grin.

"Was that supposed to be a compliment or– never mind. Jules," he points his beer bottle at me, "what're you drinking?"

"You got any scotch?"

"Ah, that's right, you and my grandpa," he mocks lightheartedly.

"Your grandpa has good taste," I tell him.

"That he does. How about Johnnie?" he offers, setting down the tequila and pulling up a bottle of Gold Label Johnnie Walker from under the table.

"Perfect," I approve, wide-eyed. I take off my jacket and add it to a pile of coats on an armchair nearby.

"Neat, right?" he confirms.

"Yeah, nice memory," I praise. He pours me a cup of booze and writes "Julia" on the side with a black sharpie. Jerrod's family may be insufferably rich, but that doesn't make Jerrod unique at our school. What *does* make him unique is his circumstantial generosity. He teeters right between "spoiled brat" and "Mother Teresa" on the selflessness scale. He'll buy the person behind him a coffee but won't tip the barista. He recycles greasy pizza boxes. Every time he flies in his family jet, he pays to have fifty trees planted in a forest. In a way, his efforts remind me of Lillian's fashion sense— he's like the second-hand clothing paired with Cartier bracelets of human beings. Neither Jerrod nor Lillian want to actually commit to each other, which only makes them more perfect together.

"Here you go." Jerrod hands me the cup.

"Thank you," I tell him and take a drink of what most people my age might mistake for gasoline if consumed. The smoky spices melt through my mouth and slowly sink down my throat with a soft sting. I savor the sensation.

When I look back to Lillian, she's pouring a shot of tequila.

"Want one, Jules?" she offers, pointing to an empty shot glass next to her own.

"No, thanks, I'd better stick to whiskey," I tell her, holding up my cup. I don't want to get drunk yet. When things start to go numb, that's when my fun ends.

Lillian pours Jerrod a shot in the glass, and they tap them on the table once and empty the contents into their mouths.

"Uhhh, that burned!" Lillian complains, shaking her head and sticking a slice of lime between her pursed pink lips. I smile and take another sip from my cup.

Jerrod, Lillian and I prattle by the bar table for a while and then boogie our way to the dance floor after the two of them choke down another shot. Lillian's dance moves are nearly as horrendous as the modern pop music booming from Jerrod's concert-grade speakers. It's awfully endearing to watch her stand there, her legs widely stanced, pointed slightly inward, while she pumps her fists in the air. She does, however, accumulate an impressive amount of momentum in her tit region, which may distract Jerrod from the awkward fist pumping just enough to get her laid tonight. Predictably, after six or so tit-bouncing songs, Jerrod leans into Lillian and whispers something into her ear. Blushing, Lillian brings her polished fingers to her mouth, suppressing a giggle, and nods "yes". She then turns to me.

"Will you be okay if I… step away for a bit?" she asks out of politeness.

"Of course," I assure her.

She takes Jerrod's hand and leads him to his bedroom upstairs, but not before swiping the Patron from the fake bar on her way up. I decide this would be a good time to explore.

I exit the sitting room and enter the foyer. A few feet past the right side of the staircase, down a hall, I turn into a dining room, where there are significantly fewer people. There's no alcohol being served, but there is, however, a competitive game of

drunk Jenga occurring over a large dinner table. I
float through the room and into the kitchen, just as a
ginger in khakis hits his head on an antique
chandelier while attempting to dislodge a game piece
from an optimally creative perspective. I hear a
cascade of crisp clicks followed by a taunting roar of
celebration from the players as the Jenga bricks
presumably tumble down.

The kitchen is significantly more modern
than the rest of the property and is amusingly clean,
leading me to question the frequency of its use. A
few girls huddle around a bowl of chips like animals
at a watering hole. They give me a censorious once-
over and say nothing. *Don't worry*, I think to myself,
I'm not here for your snacks. I imagine them in their lacy
cropped camisoles and gold hoop earrings clawing at
each other in a stretch of tall grass over a final kettle
chip at the bottom of the bowl.

I hide my amusement at this imagery as I
duck through another door across the kitchen, which
opens to a hallway on the left side of the main
staircase. I hurry down the hall, past a couple making

out, and duck through a half-closed door that would probably have been locked if not for the lack of doorknobs in the vicinity.

Behind the door is a room that I can only describe as somewhere I'm not supposed to be. I close the door gently, as much as I can, to prevent any interference with my exploring. There is still a small crack of stale light peeking through a sliver of space and the hole where the knob should sit. It shoots across the room, grazing a large desk with several objects resting on its surface. I approach the desk and set my nearly empty cup on a block of sticky notes at the corner closest to me, so as to not leave any scotch residue on the polished wood. I then tiptoe around to the back of the desk and plop myself into a throne-like leather chair.

In front of the sticky notes, on the right side of the desk, I observe a few stacks of illegible papers and a glass paperweight that encapsulates some type of mummified bug. To the left, I make out a crystal carafe containing some kind of brown liquor, a framed photo of the Kaminski family, and a vase of fountain pens. I move on to the drawers, which are all locked except for one. Inside are some silver paper clips, an assortment of sailboat-printed stamps, a tube of Chapstick, a stapler, some double-sticky tape, and an obnoxiously elegant letter opener.

I pick up the bronze paper slicer and hold it up to the streak of light that breaks through the dizzying darkness of the room. It's old as a soul, and I can see now it used to be silver, but it's tarnished. The entirety of the tool is only about four inches long and is designed to look like a feather, with small grooves cut into the body of the blade and the handle dainty and petite. I wonder what kind of bird it was meant to belong to. Maybe a metallic phoenix. *Out of ash, I rise.* I press the pointed tip to my index finger, and with a pinch, it brings me back from any whiskey wonderland I'd been experiencing. It's not enough. I press harder. The blade breaks through my skin like ice cracking on a lake. A small drop of blood swells at the peak of my finger. I watch the blood coat the end of the feather and feel a little lighter. That's when I hear the music.

It's not rap or pop, but classical: a piano. It's close, but muffled, like a small voice in my ear whispering something innocent and encouraging. I listen, still as a stone, and briefly wonder if I'm imagining the tune, but then I hear a sudden sour note, followed by a low "Dammit."

I stand up, startled, and realize I've missed something in exploring the study—a door with a knob.

I carefully close the desk drawer, creep out from behind the desk and to the back of the room, and press my ear against the frame.

Sure enough, a moment later, the music restarts. It's a blue song, with hints of magenta and speckles of green that weave in and out, mixing through the tune like cinnamon and honey in milk. It makes me sad and happy and drunk and sober all at once, and I'm so moved that I only feel the music and nothing else. Not even the letter cutter, which I forget I'm holding, carelessly slipping from my hand. It lands with a clank right at the foot of the door. The piano playing stops.

I snatch the bronze feather up from the ground and hold my breath, which is subsequently knocked from my body as the door is flung open into my side, and I topple over onto the floor of the Kaminski family study.

"Bloody hell, are you alright?!" a male voice asks, urgently.

"Never better" I mumble with whatever breath is left in me. My knee glows with pain and I feel a bruise blooming where its cap cushioned my fall.

"Oh my God, I just hit a girl with a door. I am so sorry." He remarks in such a panic that it doesn't sound English.

"No, really, I'm okay; I really am. Don't worry." I console my perpetrator as I start to sit up.

"Are you sure? Are you hurt?" he asks as he approaches me. "Oh my god, look at your knee," he says, crouching down to me. He puts a big hand on my raspberried leg, but I don't look at my kneecap; I just look at him.

He meets my eyes with his own and pulls back his hand. "Hey, wait, I think I know you. You might not remember me, but I think I saw you earlier today, I just started working at–"

"The Coffee Shop," I say, interrupting the new barista.

"Yeah, that's right," he says, pleasantly surprised. "It was Julia, right?" he asks. Now it's my turn to be surprised.

"I'm sorry, I don't remember your name," I tell him.

"That's all right; I don't recall telling it to you. It's Max," he says, sounding very British.

"Well it's nice to meet you, officially, Max."

"You as well. I'm sorry it had to be by my clocking you with a door." He sounds embarrassed.

"Oh, it's seriously okay, it's really my fault for standing there like that in the first place."

"Well, you didn't hit yourself with a door… Do you mind me asking what exactly you were doing there?"

I consider coming up with a less intrusive reason I was crouched by the door, but I'm too flustered to think up a lie. "I was listening to the piano music," I admit.

"Were you now?" He pauses, then asks, "Well, what did you think?"

"It was beautiful," I say.

"Really?" he asks, sitting down on the floor next to me. As he gets situated, I shove the bloodied letter opener in my purse as subtly as possible, unsure of where else to put it.

"Yes, it was," I confirm.

"Well, that's good to hear. You're actually the first person to hear that one," he tells me, with a hint of nervousness in his voice.

"Wait, did you write that?" I ask in disbelief.

"I did," he tells me, his eyes humbly pointed at the ground.

"Are you a composer?"

"Only by night," he jokes, "by day I'm a lowly MBA student."

This makes me smile. "I'm guessing we go to the same school then, if you're working at the coffee shop across the street from campus," I say.

"Periodically. I'm normally in London, but I'm studying abroad here next semester, and I'm already on break," he says.

"And you thought you'd come here early to get a jump on campus life?"

"That, as well as campus expenses. I have to pay the international student's tuition. But my mum is originally from Massachusetts, so I'm technically a US citizen, meaning I'm allowed to work—hence the coffee shop gig," he explains.

"Got it. And how do you know Jerrod?"

"I didn't until tonight. My roommate said some guys from the 'soccer' club invited us," he says, putting the word *soccer* in quotations with his fingers.

"Are they still here?" I ask.

"Not sure, I stumbled in here during my search for the bathroom, and circled back for a go at the piano afterwards."

"Well, I'll let you get back to your friends,"
I say.

"I don't particularly want to. I'm quite
enjoying talking to you," he says. Blush splashes
across my cheeks, and I can't help but smile.

"What are you studying?" he asks, sparing
me from my unwarranted embarrassment.

"I'm getting my master's degree in fine arts,
studying poetry," I tell him.

"Do you want to be a writer?" he asks.

"I suppose," I say, unsure about how to tell
him I don't really *want* to be anything.

"That's cool, what do you like to write
about?"

"Mostly short form prose."

"About?" he repeats.

No one had ever asked me what I like to
write *about*. In fact, I hadn't even asked myself this
question. I instinctually cock my head to the side like
an idiot and think about my answer. After a few too
many seconds, I blurt something out.

"The beauty in pain." As soon as the words leave my mouth, I cringe. Max looks pensive.

"Wow, that's…"

"A lot, I know," I say, trying to think of a way to talk about something else.

"No— well, I mean, yes, but in a good way," he says warmly. I squint at him with curious relief, and he continues speaking. "I mean there's a certain escape in the act of suffering that I think can absolutely be beautiful— like how a really beautiful piano song can also be sad. People don't smile when they're most moved by a beautiful song; they weep," he says.

"Do you think it's because they're in pain?" I ask him.

"I think maybe it's because they see the beauty in life and in death, even if there is pain present, and this is a lot to feel at once."

"It's funny how something as simple as a short song can make people think about life and death so deeply," I remark.

"Well, think of it this way: If life were a song, what we live would be the crescendo, and death is the climax. Death really moves people– and it's not only about loss. It's also about the beauty of everything that came before. The climax of a song feels like a moment of perfect glory, a 'final hurrah,' if you will, honoring life, even if it is a bit tragic," he says, "like a swan song, if you will."

"A what?" I ask.

"A swan song – it's an old wise tale that a swan, before it dies, sings a final beautiful note honoring life. It's been turned into a metaphor for a final performance symbolizing the loss of someone or something."

"So, when beauty is present in an emotional, sad, or painful moment, it reminds people that some of the most beautiful things in life can happen in pain's wake? And feeling these feelings is beautiful?" I clarify.

"Yeah, at least that's one way to look at it. What do you think?" he asks.

I pause. "I think that loss brings the truest pain. Sometimes finding the beauty in pain is the only way to move forward. Maybe people find comfort in that suffering. If you can't find comfort in suffering, whether that be in glory, beauty or something else, what do you have left?"

He looks forward into the darkness, his lips parted in concentration, searching for an answer to my hypothetical question. After what seems like careful consideration he meets my gaze with a calm confidence and speaks a single word.

"Hope."

4.

ope. It was something about the way he said it that made me feel like I was understanding what the word meant for the first time. I wanted to be able to laugh at him for his foolish optimism, or to lecture him on just how desperately hopeless life really was. I wanted to tell him that the only way to control your suffering was to orchestrate it. That the only true pleasure in life must be found in pain, because if you master pain you will not even need to hope for anything at all. But the way he said that one word, spoken with so much strength, and trust, there in the dark, has left me speechless. Unable to tell him any of this, I just stare at him, wondering what he has that is worth hoping for with such a genuine drive, that even I would question the safety of my own suffering.

Then, without warning, something eclipses the door, blocking the light beam from entering the room. Through the empty doorknob hole, it spoke.

"Why don't you guys make out already?" it says in a crude manner, one in which only the person speaking the words might find them amusing. And although this voice seldom speaks in full, coherent sentences, I still recognize the distinctive, low and gravelly phonetics of its owner.

"Henry." I say, flatly. The door swings open. In the doorway is the beefy outline of Henry Langmore.

"Julia? Who's this twink?" he asks with a chuckle.

"Shut up, Henry," I say, getting up from the ground, taking my cup from the desk, and pushing past him into the hallway. Max follows my lead, standing up and extending a hand to Henry.

"My name is Max. You must be Henry?" he tells him calmly.

"Right on, British twink!" Henry says and daps him up, instead of shaking his hand as Max likely intended.

"Right, I'm sure alcohol can cloud our judgment, but I must say, I would prefer it if you wouldn't use such a derogatory term," Max tells him.

"Bro, I don't even understand what you're saying—was that even English?" Henry hides from his incomprehension behind mockery.

"I'm asking that you don't use the word 'twink'," Max says firmly. "If I *were* gay, it would be quite offensive."

Finally understanding, a testosterone-fueled fire is set ablaze in Henry's eyes. He sets his beer on the stairs and takes a step towards Max, lengthening his back so that he's almost eye to eye with him. "Oh," he says, getting up in Max's face, "would you look at that, I hurt the twink's feelings."

"Listen, I was just making a suggestion. If you want to be an asshole, that's on you," Max says bravely.

"All right, well I'll stay an asshole, and you can stay one big ol' twink!" Henry barks in Max's face.

"You guys look like you're about to kiss," a fresh voice observes from the staircase. It's Lillian, stumbling down from Jerrod's room. Her observation detonates Henry. He forcefully shoves Max away from him with a revolted huff.

Instead of fighting back, Max simply scoffs in disbelief. Shaking his head in disgust and glaring at Henry, he backs up towards the front door and turns to leave, but then looks back one last time.

"It was nice talking to you, Julia," he says to me. "I'm sorry the night had to take such an unsavory turn."

"Max," I say softly, but he doesn't respond. He leaves the party and the house suddenly feels very empty.

"What a faggot." Henry laughs behind me. A hollow anger swims in my heart.

Without hesitating, I spin around and lay a passionate slap on Henry's face. Several surrounding voices chant a low *oooohhhh* in response. But humiliating Henry only helps so much.

I down what little scotch is left in my cup, but it fails to extinguish my rage. I set the cup on the stairs with a disgruntled crunch and stride for the exit. Lillian drunkenly calls after me, but I ignore her and dive through the door, down the stairs, and into the night.

Outside, I look around. Max is long gone. Cold air gnaws at my exposed skin, and a violent shiver scampers up my spine and branches across my shoulders. I consider going back for my jacket, but I'm too flustered. The heat of the moment will have to do. I start off down the sidewalk towards my apartment, but I only make it a few steps before a strong hand hooks onto my arm and reels me backward, halting my progress. I whirl around and flash a threatening glare up at Henry. His fingers burrow into my arm, and a warm pinch pumps through my limb. I stand my ground, but I don't resist his iron grip. I just look at him with a dreadful, angry attraction. He looks at me with a cannibal grin.

"That was hot," he says hungrily. I know he's referring to the slap. He hands me my coat.

I've only ever seen Henry in athletic clothes and no clothes. If he wore belts, I would ask him to hit me with those, but he doesn't wear belts, so he just uses his leathery hands, which do just fine. Now, as I straddle him on his bed, with my tongue in his mouth, he paddles a particularly spicy smack into my ass with both his hands, and without pulling away, squeezes my bare cheeks hard, like lemons. A juicy sting rushes through me. I engrave his back with my nails as he bobs me up and down. Then, he wraps one arm around my torso, and weaves his other hand through a handful of hair on my head and stands up and flips me over onto my back. He lowers his head to my breasts, nibbling and sucking on my nipples till they're throbbing and raw. Then he straightens up, and lifts my right knee up next to my shoulder, and holds my opposite left arm down into the bed by the wrist. He pumps in and out of me with a stabbing intensity and I sink my teeth into my shoulder. A great wave pulses through me.

When we're done, I open Henry's dresser and rummage around until I find a comfy looking gray T-shirt, printed with a crimson college soccer logo.

"Can I sleep in this?" I ask, holding it up from the drawer to show him.

"You can keep that. It doesn't fit me anyway, it's from freshman year."

"I didn't know you played soccer," I remark, sliding my arms through the bottom opening in preparation to pull it on. I observe that the T-shirt's tag says it's a men's size medium.

"I didn't," he hesitated, "It was a friend's."

The way he says the word *friend* feels dark, like a secret.

———————————————————

When I wake up the next morning, I'm alone in Henry's bed. As I start to sit upright, a small headache graces me with its presence. I rub my eyes, exit the covers, and head for the bathroom. There, I use some minty mouthwash and turn on the shower. I take off the soccer T-shirt, step under the hot flow of water, and let it hold me in a burning hug. I wash my face, but not my hair, because, as suspected, Henry's shampoo is indeed the type that lightens hair, and I don't think I'd look very good blonde.

When I get out of the shower, I can't find a bath towel, so I dry off with the one meant for your hands. I run it up my calves and thighs, wrap it around my waist and chest, and dab off my arms and neck. As I watch myself scrunch the towel through my hair in the mirror, I notice that on my shoulder is a purple constellation of small bruises in the oblong pattern of my bite. I trace its entirety with my fingers.

I make Henry's bed and begin the quest for my clothes. When I locate all the articles and my purse, I check my phone and see that it's 10 AM and I have six missed calls from Lillian. A gust of guilt sweeps through me and rattles my conscience. I restore my pants and shirt to my body in record time.

Then I slide into my wedges and coat and rush through Henry's apartment door, putting my phone to my ear on my way out. It rings once.

"Jules?" Lillian asks eagerly.

"Yes, hi! It's me!" I confess, rushing down the stairwell.

"Oh thank god, I was worried Boston PD was going to be on the other side! You disappeared into thin air last night!"

"I know, I'm sorry I missed your calls. I went back to Henry's place, and we got carried away."

"After *that* smack?"

"Yeah, we, uh, worked it out," I admit, exiting the building.

"Well, shit, you should work for the UN or something because that must've been some peace treaty," she jokes. "What happened in the first place?"

"It's a long story," I warn her.

"Try me. Let's meet at The Coffee Shop in an hour," Lillian suggests.

"Um… let's try somewhere new today."

Lillian agrees to meet me at a brunch spot near campus. I stop by my apartment, change into some jeans and a T-shirt, take my pill, run a brush through my hair, and put on some sneakers. I almost forget to grab the basil plant I bought her the evening prior to replace the one Bean ate. On my way to brunch, I log the events from the night before. The cute guy from The Coffee Shop, whose name is Max, was at the party. He goes to my school. He writes music and plays piano. He's gregariously intelligent from what I've gathered. He was flirting with me… or was he?

"Oh my God, are you stupid? He totally was!" Lillian says to me when I tell her all this.

"Then why did he leave?" I ask without thinking.

"Because would you want the first thing you do at your new school to be getting in a fight? No!" she argues, accidentally kicking the table and ruffling the leaves of her new plant.

"I guess not," I agree.

A waiter comes and plops down an avocado toast for Lillian and some huevos rancheros for me.

"Thanks," I say, adding some chili flakes.

When the waiter is gone, Lillian asks, "Wait, so if you had such a good time with Max, why did you fuck the homophobe that scared him away?"

"I'm not really sure," I lie.

"You confuse me sometimes," she says before taking a big bite of her toast. "So what are you going to do about Max?" she asks with her mouth full.

"I don't know what there is to do," I say, picking at my eggs.

"Give him your number or something! You know where to find him!" she points out.

"What? No. I don't like him like that; we just had a nice conversation, that's all. Plus, if he wanted my number, he would've asked for it," I counter.

"In between hitting you with a door, discussing life and death itself and almost getting punched in the face? I mean the night wasn't exactly super chill."

"I don't know," I tell her.

"Why is it so hard for you to accept that a hot, nice, smart guy is probably into you? Instead you go home with roid-raging Henry Langmore," she says, sounding frustrated and rolling her eyes.

"I'm not—I don't know; I just don't see it. Me, of all people?" I say, trying to comprehend why Max would be interested in me.

"I mean are you fucking with me? You're one of the most laid-back, real and considerate people that I know. And you're *hot!* If I didn't know you better I'd think you were acting oblivious for attention or something."

"I'm not, I'm sorry," I tell her truthfully. I hate stressing out Lillian.

"I know, because I *do* know you better. You don't have to say 'sorry'. I just love you and I want to see you happy."

"I love you too, Lil, thank you."

She smiles at me.

"What're you up to for the rest of the day?"
she asks. *Bless her short attention span*, I think.

"I have to buy a copy of *The Bell Jar*."

5.

I *felt very still and very empty, the way the eye of a tornado must feel, moving dully along in the middle of the surrounding hullabaloo.* I read from the final page of *The Bell Jar's* first chapter. From my corner in the library, I tint the outskirts of the book's pages red, as I habitually slit my fingers across the paper's razor-thin edges. The zesty sting encourages me to continue reading. When each of my fingertips is properly decorated with clusters of small cuts, I pinch them against my thumb, coaxing an aching sensation from the openings as I push through the words on the pages. When roughly the first third of the pages are coated in scarlet, I decide to make the cloudy walk home. I cross to the opposite side of the street when I come upon The Coffee Shop, pushing Max from my mind.

Fish swims in circles with delight, when I'm back. I pretend it's out of love. I give him a couple pellets, just for being cute. Then, I wash some dishes, water my plants, and get ready for bed. It's only 8:30 PM, but it feels like midnight. I take off my jeans and lay down in my sheets and watch the sunset through my open bedroom door, glowing through the kitchen windows, as I drift off to sleep.

This time, instead of Lilac, my dress is white and boxy, like everything else in the room. My arms are no longer spotless, but dotted with freckles and crossed with cuts. I sit on the edge of a small bed. A sterile fluorescent light buzzes in my ears and makes the space between my skull and my brain itchy.

"Julia," a female voice says, and I look up at a woman, also dressed in white, holding a clipboard and sitting across from me on a stool. "How are you feeling today?" she asks.

A terrible foreign numbness sits thick in me. "I feel nothing," I say.

"That's good, Julia; that means the medication we gave you is working," she tries to reassure me.

"Where's my mom?" I ask. My face feels like cotton.

"She's downstairs, in the lobby. You can see her in a little bit," she tells me.

"I don't want to see her," I tell the nurse. I try to move my hands from the bed, but my limbs feel limp and puny and don't respond to my commands.

"Why is that? Did she hurt you?" she asks.

"She would never," I tell her. Agitated, I try harder now to move but remain lodged in this vulnerable purgatory between gravity and whatever medication they've pumped into me. Suddenly, a hot, choking sadness breathes down my neck, and I'm overcome with emotion. "I want to see my dad," I burst into sobs.

"Is that why you hurt yourself? Because you want to see him again?" she asks with professional empathy.

"I miss him," I cry, "I miss him so much."

Grief torments me. I begin to claw at the sides of my thighs, but I panic when all I feel is a soft static. No matter how hard I try and scratch, I'm still buried in this dense absent feeling. I cry louder.

"I know Julia, but I need you to stop hurting yourself for me. Can you do that?"

I shake my head as much as I can manage. "I can't. I want to, but I can't. I can't stop it," I wail.

The nurse looks at me apologetically, then pushes a button on a small electronic box strung around her neck. Seconds later, two brawley men in blue scrubs enter the room, take hold of my lanky arms and legs and stick them to the bed while the nurse jabs a shot into my thigh. For a fleeting moment, I find relief in the pinch. A blinding flash blares in front of me and then fades to a tranquil black.

I open my eyes to a sultry darkness. Shaking, I blindly feel my way to the lamp on my bedside dresser. I switch on the light and sit back into a ball on my bed and rub my palms into my moist eyelids. Then I wrap my arms around myself in a protective hug. Everything is quiet with the exception of my heavy, trembling breath. *I felt very still and very empty.*

But then, suddenly, the tornado Plath described in her book isn't moving around me— it moves throughout me, rearranging my insides, eating them and spitting them back out in all the wrong places. I feel misaligned, disoriented, like I'm floating underwater, needing to rise for air, but unable to differentiate up from down. A choking tension grows in my chest. This feeling turns in me, stewing in my neck, back, and thighs. I want to run from myself. *I want to but I can't. I can't stop it.* From my seated fetal position, I start kneading my arms, gripping my way down my ribs and waist. Then, I move my hands to squeeze at my thighs. I want to pop them like balloons. I pinch and stretch my latex skin but it only inflates my panic and elevates my desire for a grounding reprise. I start to dig at the sides of my legs, slowly filling my nails with skin. I excavate the ease. I carve out the comfort. I paint deep ruby gashes across the canvas of my epidermis. A colorful burning peels away at layers of my fear, but still, I can't scratch the core of this pitiful itch.

Frustrated, I leave my bed. I know I should just try to go back to sleep. *I can't.* I pace around my room, my hands on my head, like a guilty convict, before dizzily entering the bathroom. There, next to the sink, right where I left it, is my hair iron. I put my hands on the counter, breathing in slow, drawn-out huffs, in a futile attempt to reason with my irrational cravings. I suppress a whimper and plug in the iron. This failure, to resist these urges, burdens me nearly as much as the reasons I commit these forbidden acts. But without this beautiful pain, there would be no memory of love in my past. There would be no escape from myself in the present. Tears cloud my vision. *I miss him so much.* I snatch the iron from the counter, take a knee on my bathroom floor, and plunge the searing surface into my thigh.

A dazzling firework erupts through me as I purge the distress from my being. I fill my lungs with sweet relief. Finally, my discomfort dissipates as the bubbling heat melts into my skin. I feel light as a feather. Sparkling stars materialize before my eyes. I discard the iron, and sink to the ground.

I lay on the cool tile of my bathroom floor for a short eternity, and when I see the makings of dawn through my bedroom window, I crawl back to my bed. The gentle beat of a pulsing burn lulls me to sleep.

I wake up to a knocking, seemingly coming from outside my apartment door. The pale midday sun shames me. I have no doubt missed my morning classes. I confirm my suspicions when I sit up and see that my phone's clock reads 12:30 PM. I once again have a procession of missed calls from Lillian. As I'm tenderly pulling on a pair of pj shorts over my shredded thighs, I hear the rapping at the door again, this time followed by the muffled, good-humored voice of Lillian shouting, "Open up, sleeping beauty!"

I'm struck with remorse when I realize she probably had her coffees alone. I hustle across my room and living area and swing open the door. Lillian stands in front of my entrance, wearing her sunglasses on the top of her head, a pair of black and white checkered jeans, and a pink knit sweater.

"Welfare check, and not the money kind, sorry!" She announces her arrival with her arms outstretched, and a smile spread across her face, presenting herself like a gift. She rushes forward and hugs me. "Are you okay?" She whispers.

"Yeah, I just had a long night. I'm so sorry for leaving you all alone for coffee." I apologize.

"That was the least of my worries! What happened?"

I hesitate. "I had a nightmare and couldn't sleep, so I guess I slept in."

"Is that all that happened?" she asks, pulling away from our embrace and taking my shoulders between her hands. I just stare at her, guilty. I know she knows. She's watched this pattern of habits unfold before. She can smell it in the air, like rain before it falls. Neither of us wants to believe it's happening again. I watch, ashamed, as she hesitantly scans my body. When her eyes are alerted to the damage on my legs, they erupt with tears.

"Oh, Julia," she cries, alarmed at the sight of my injuries. I let her into my apartment and close the door. She takes my arm and leads me to my bathroom.

"First things first, we need to clean this," she says, wiping her eyes and sitting me down on the closed lid of my toilet. "Where do you keep your medicine stuff?"

I point to a drawer under the sink. She pulls out the compartment, rummages around, and cracks open a box of untouched band-aids and lays a handful on the counter.

"Lillian, you don't have to do this."

"I know I don't *have* to. But let's be real, who else is going to take care of you?"

"I'm an adult; I should take care of myself," I acknowledge.

"Well, maybe you *should*, but that doesn't mean you *will*. And that's not meant to be mean. It's just how things are when you're stressed out like this."

"I'm sorry Lil, I want to stop doing this, I really do," I say, sitting with my arms crossed, avoiding eye contact.

"Okay, you don't need to apologize, but you also can't keep telling me you want to stop hurting yourself and doing nothing about it," she says, pulling the cap off a saline spray bottle.

She bends down to where my blistering burn basks on my left thigh and mists it with the salty solution. I wince with pleasure as the saline seeps into my injury. Lillian must sense my delight. She stares at me with incomprehensible concern, like she might begin to cry again.

"You're right," I agree.

"Do we need to make you an appointment with your psychiatrist?" she suggests, fanning above my burn with her hand to dry the spray.

"I guess so," I solemnly give in.

"Okay, let me put these on, and then I'll call them." Lillian says peeling apart the waxy preservative seal from the first bandage. She dresses my wound with four band-aids. Then she hands me an antiseptic cream. "Here, rub this on your scratches, and I'll call Campus Health."

I feel a pinch in my free hand and see that I've dug my nails deep into my palms and left behind small moon shaped indents. I sit on my toilet feeling like one big failure. I can't function and I can't successfully hide this fact. I'm a colossal burden. I'm the tornado from *The Bell Jar*. I sit there at the center of my own destructive universe and upend the lives of the people I love. Lillian pops her head back in the room.

"They said the earliest they can get you is three months from now, which is bullshit. Also, I'm staying here tonight. Let me go get my stuff and feed Bean and I'll be right back." *Case in point*, I think.

Lillian and I spend the rest of the day doing homework at my kitchen table. Against my better judgment, I decide to resume reading *The Bell Jar*.

Maybe it's due to the fact that I massively rid my system of angst the night before, or because of Lillian's moral support, but the book is significantly more palatable today. Despite its slow but steady increase in depressive tension, the main character, Esther Greenwood, is actually quite hilarious and relatable at that. I finish the second third of the novel, only minimally chewing my lips and cheeks as I go. When the sun starts to set, and we're tired of working, Lillian and I order Chinese food and flip on the TV. Lillian skips through channels until she finds a floofy Hallmark Christmas movie. She turns to me.

"Are you going back to Maine for Christmas?" she asks between mouthfuls of noodles.

"I'm not sure; David is Jewish, so my mom doesn't really do Christmas anymore," I say, picking at my spicy chicken.

"I mean, your stepdad can celebrate Hanukkah, and you can still go see your family," she points out.

"I guess it's just felt weird ever since my mom got remarried," I admit.

"Cause they're not your traditions?" she clarifies.

"Maybe, but mostly because I just don't really fit in anywhere. It was the same way at Thanksgiving. My mom is glued to David, my step-siblings have each other, and I'm sort of just there because I should be, but I don't really want to be," I confess.

"Do you want to come back to New York with me?" she offers.

"Maybe." I smile at the idea of getting to spend Christmas with Lillian.

"Think about it; it would be fun," she tells me, but the notion of imposing on her more than I already have is upsetting, so I simply tuck the thought away. Just then, I feel my phone buzz. Henry Langmore's name glows across my phone screen. I remove it from the notifications bar without responding to it. Lillian and I finish our dinner and the movie and fall asleep in my bed.

6.

The next morning, I will myself to wake up for class, then take a shower and choke down a protein bar before my pill, to imitate some form of normalcy. When Lillian is satisfied with my performance, I'm cleared for class and we walk to campus.

"Okay, I have to feed Bean and then shower before my afternoon class, so I probably can't get coffee today. Will you be okay by yourself?" Lillian asks when we make it to the building my seminar is in.

"Yeah, of course, I'm feeling a lot better. Thanks for staying with me last night," I tell her, forcing my enthusiasm.

"Anytime, Jules. If you want me to come back, just call me," she offers.

Although appreciative, I lie through my teeth, "I will."

When my class is over, I find myself habitually navigating my way to The Coffee Shop. I decide that despite the awkward encounter that awaits my arrival, I can't avoid the place forever. I remind myself that what Henry said to Max wasn't my fault, but it's not just about that. What I'm really avoiding aren't just feelings of responsibility for Max's unfortunate experience. I'm also dodging an interaction with my own dumb gooey feelings for him. Whatever hope Max had expressed there at the party hadn't been contagious enough to stick, and I'm worried if I see him again, he'll infect me with it for good. I've lost enough hope in my lifetime to learn it only leads to disappointment. That's why I keep to the reliability of pain.

I make it to The Shop's block, and I already find myself affected by the simple idea of seeing Max again, as I unconsciously check to see how my hair looks in the window of a deli down the street. *Don't be stupid*, I remind my silly heart, which beats as if it's a small cage housing a dozen nervous hummingbirds. I push my body through the door and hop in line, risking eye contact with no one as I keep my gaze on the floor. When I muster the courage to look up, I'm pleasantly disappointed. Max is not at the checkout. I get my espresso and sit down at my table in the corner and breathe a sigh of sad relief. What a funny feeling it is to narrowly avoid the chaos of talking to someone you really did want to talk to. I sip my coffee and sift through the words on the pages of *The Bell Jar*.

After a few chapters of this, a strong shadow appears in my peripheral vision. I look up from my book, with nervous light in my eyes. Max stands over me, next to my table.

"Hey," he greets me with a shy smile. A small white cup is nested in his big hands.

"Max, hi," I say back warmly. I feel a rosiness pooling in my cheeks as I resist admiring his handsome features.

"Hey," he says again. "I, uh, wanted to give you this on the house." He extends the to-go cup to me. "Maybe it'll help make up for my storming out on you the other night. I'm really sorry about that; I just didn't want my first impression here to be 'the guy that gets in fights at parties.'"

"Oh, I understand, you don't even have to apologize, let alone bring me a…" I gesture to the cup.

"An espresso, like you ordered last time," he tells me, "but this one's decaffeinated, cause I saw you'd already had one." His thoughtfulness moves me.

I take the cup from his hand. "Thank you."

He nods and smiles a satisfied grin, then asks, "What are you reading?"

"Oh, just a book for class, it's called *The Bell Jar*. It's by Sylvia Plath." I say, setting down the cup. I tip the book toward him but not without subtly covering the blood-dipped pages with my fingers and burying my own dirty shame deep behind my eyes.

"Nice, I haven't read that one, but I've heard of Plath. What class are you reading it for?"

"It's a class on famous dead poets called *Dead Poets Society*," I tell him with a grin, imagining the pride Professor Bowling would feel if he were here to witness his witfully named class highlighted in conversation.

"Clever. *Dead Poets Society* – now that is a book I've read, and it happens to be one of my favorites," he says.

"Really? I haven't even seen the movie."

"You haven't? Well, that's bloody criminal! What're you doing tonight?" he asks.

"Tonight?" I confirm, hoping he's asking me what I think he's asking me.

"Yes, tonight. This is a proper emergency. I must show you this film as soon as possible," he says. I marvel at his charm.

"Well, then, I guess tonight I'm watching *Dead Poets Society*." I tell him, trying my own hand at being suave.

"Perfect. Text the number I wrote on your cup there, and I'll get back to you with a time and place," he says, winking. I look down and turn the cup, and sure enough, there is a neatly written phone number printed on the side. *One step ahead of me*, I think, impressed.

"Okay," I grin.

A female voice calls out, "Max!" from the register.

Max turns around to his manager, who is watching him sternly, with a hint of amusement.

"Are you gonna come make some coffee, or are you gonna sit around flirting all day?" she says with a hefty Boston accent.

"Sorry, Gina!" He yells back and then looks at me. "See you tonight, then." He nods, grinning with slight embarrassment at Gina's comment.

"Yeah," I say, failing to hold back a smile.

I pack up my book, swing on my backpack and take my cup. On my way out of the shop, I smile back over my shoulder at Max, who looks effortlessly charming, taking an order from a girl with dark curls. Suddenly, a gray thought moves through my head like a cloud and blocks any optimism from touching my heart.

When I get home, I pick up my phone, but I don't text the number on the cup. Instead, I call Lillian.

"Hey, I just got out of my class. What's up? Is everything okay?" she asks, a dash of concern in her tone.

"Yeah, everything's great, actually a little too great," I confess, "Max gave me his number and asked me to come over tonight."

"What?! Julia, Oh my God that's awesome! See, I told you he was into you!" Lillian squeals through the phone.

"Yeah, except… I'm not going," I tell her reluctantly.

"What the hell, Julia?! Why not?!" she asks in disbelief.

"Well, I think he's playing me. He probably gives his number to thirty girls like that every day and invites them over to 'watch a movie'."

"Hang on, I need more details. I'm coming over," she says, inviting herself to my place. "Okay," I laugh.

Ten minutes later, there's a knock on my door. When I open it, Lillian doesn't even say "Hi", and jumps right to business, marching her pinstripe pant-suited self swiftly into my apartment with such urgency that her silky yellow cravat flows around her neck and down her back

"Okay, so what the fuck happened?!" she asks, wide-eyed, while plopping her backpack down on one of my dining chairs.

"Well, he came up to me at The Coffee Shop and we got to talking about *Dead Poets Society* and he told me if I text the number he'd written on my espresso cup, we could watch it together at his place tonight." I explain, gesturing to the cup on my table.

"Oh my *God,* that's so romantic!" Lillian huffs, "So what exactly is the problem?" she asks, leaning on the table, curious, one hand on her hip and one on the chair.

"Well, he probably just wants to sleep with me."

"And that's a bad thing because…?" She sarcastically waits for me to finish her sentence.

I open my mouth to answer her question, but then I pause. It dawns on me that the only reason I would be upset if Max wanted to have me over for sex is that I want more than sex with him. I may have just compromised my position.

Lillian's patience dissolves, and she speaks for me.

"I mean you sleep with Henry all the time, and you don't even like him– Oh my God," She interrupts herself, "I knew it! You like Max and you don't want him to just want to sleep with you! You want him to like you back! That's it isn't it?" She announces her epiphany like she's solved a murder. And she's right– I'm guilty as hell. I press my lips together in a flat line across my face.

"I don't want to like him, but I think I do," I confess.

"Ha! There we are! Well, then you *have* to go!" Lillian practically screams her verdict.

"I can't; I'm just going to be setting myself up for disappointment," I object.

"Julia, he gave you his number before he even invited you over. He probably just saw an opportunity and took it. And if he *does* just want to sleep with you, you sleep with him, or don't, and move on. Big whoop! If you don't hang out with him, you'll never know whether he wants more or not." She looks at me with a knowing smile. "The only sure way you won't have something more with him is if you never text him." She picks up the cup, and holds it out to me. I take it from her hand.

A few minutes later, I get a text back from Max, summoning me to an address in North Cambridge around seven o'clock. Lillian and I performatively do homework together for a few hours, before we ravage my closet for something I can wear tonight. We settle on some jeans and a nice beige sweater that Lillian had given me last season, after it had gone out of season the season before. Then she helps me straighten my hair, likely as a precaution more so than an act of service. After this, I methodically put on some makeup, ironically attempting to appear as though I'm wearing none.

"Oooo, you clean up nicely, young lady!" Lillian tells me in her best old lady voice.

"Thanks," I laugh, putting on some sneakers, a jacket, and grabbing a canvas bag. We leave my apartment and head downstairs.

"Where are you headed?" Lillian asks when we get to the edge of the sidewalk.

"It looks like a house in North Cambridge, sort of near that one cemetery."

"Okay, be careful over there. Call me if you need anything!"

"Okay, Grandma, love you!" I joke with a wave, and start down the sidewalk in the direction my map tells me to walk.

"And have fun!" Lillian calls out after me. I smile back at her with gratitude, then continue on my way, down the frost-bitten streets.

Part 2

7.

A soft blanket of dusk settles over Boston as I walk toward Max's address. Normally, I might find the sky's display of gentle, dissolving pinks and periwinkles to be soothing, but now, they are simply background noise to my anxious inner dialogue. Thoughts race through my head, running through every possible thing that might go awry. *What if he doesn't like me?* I wonder. *What if he does?* My nerves tie themselves into knots and sit hot and sticky in my stomach, rising in intensity by the minute, like dough. I'm not used to this—*not* wanting to feel. I imagine this is the sentiment a racehorse might experience just before the gun—pinned, fired up, ready to bolt. I need to let loose.

I check my map to see how much further I have to go and conveniently see a liquor store further along my route. Alcohol might be a good way to sedate myself. I stop in and grab a bottle of red wine, as whiskey doesn't feel appropriate. It *clanks* awkwardly in the canvas bag against my bony hip as I arrive at a small, brown, haunted-looking house with a chicken wire fence and a patchy yard.

I look down at my phone and compare the address to the one Max texted me, suspicious I've come to the wrong place, but there's been no obvious mistake. I tuck my phone back in my pocket, pry open the rusted gateway, climb a few creaky stairs, and thump timidly twice on the door with my knuckles. It opens a few seconds later to Max's shining face.

"Hi," he says cheerfully, "Welcome to my mansion." He holds the door open for me and I smile and follow his lead.

"Thank you," I say, trying my best to prevent my voice from shaking with giddy awkwardness.

"It's nothing special, but it's enough." He gestures around him awkwardly. As inhospitable as the house should feel, I feel oddly at home as Max guides me through a dark narrow hallway, into a small, smoky kitchen.

Scattered across a foldable table are two miniature round candles with the star of David printed on the side, placed thoughtfully around a plate of grapes, a stack of cut up pre-sliced cheese and some Ritz crackers. Next to the plate are two coffee mugs and a bottle of red wine. The whole setup is incredibly charming. I can't contain my amusement.

"Are those Shabbat candles?" I ask with a giggle.

"Yeah, they're my roommate's. It's the best I could do. I wanted to take you out for a drink, but I don't get paid until the end of the month, so that will have to wait until next week," he says with an embarrassed laugh.

"I think it's perfect," I tell him. "In fact, you're actually one step ahead of me," I say, pulling out my own red wine from my bag.

"Well, would you look at that!" he remarks, a sprinkle of relief in his tone.

I set the bottle on his kitchen counter next to a dish-drying rack and move to set my coat over one of the two mismatched wicker patio chairs.

"Please," Max says, pulling out the less tattered seat, "allow me." He takes my coat and drapes it over the back of the chair and then motions for me to sit.

"Wow, to what do I owe this exceptional chivalry?" I ask, mostly joking. As charmed as I am, I can't ignore the slight suspicion that this is all a calculated act, seeking some kind of sexual applause.

"Well, maybe the Americans call it 'exceptional chivalry', but the Brits call it 'basic first date etiquette'." He winks and I blush at his referring to the night as a date.

"Madame," he says, comically screwing the cap off the bottle as if he's been rudely distracted, "tonight we have the finest screw-off red wine in the discounted aisle of the liquor store. Please enjoy." He puts a hand behind his back, imitating a waiter, and splashes the dark purple liquid into my unorthodox drinking vessel.

"Thank you." I laugh, take the mug awkwardly and scan my surroundings for something to talk about, as the air fills with candle smoke and nervous energy. I spot the words *Woodford Boxing Center* printed in forest green on the porcelain, above a small graphic of two boxing gloves crossed over each other.

"Are you a boxer?" I ask.

"Well, I can't be running around looking like a 'twink' without something to show for it, can I now?" he jokes, filling his own plain baby yellow mug.

I exhale a single small breath of laughter at his good-humored reference to Henry's past insult.

"Cheers." He clinks his mug into mine and we both take a drink. It tastes like someone combined rubbing alcohol with grape juice and added too much sugar. I drink it anyway.

"How long have you been doing that?" I ask between nervous sips.

"Drinking?" he jokes.

"Boxing," I smile.

"Oh, years. I started in sixth form, when I was sixteen."

"Nice, what inspired that?" I ask.

"Well, my parents had just gotten divorced and I needed something to take my mind off things. Plus, the gym was right down the street from me."

"You grew up in… Woodford, then?" I assume, reading the name on the mug. I'd prefer to steer our conversation away from the topic of parents.

"That's right, in London. Where did you grow up?" he asks.

"Cape Elizabeth, in Maine," I respond.

"I've heard of it. Do you play any sports?"

"Not anymore. I used to ride horses when I was younger," I say, then pop a grape in my mouth and force it down my tight throat out of respect.

"That's nice, believe it or not, I've never ridden one before."

"Really? That's okay; I wouldn't worry too much; it's pretty overrated."

"Yeah? I suppose I'm not too worried, but I would still like to try it at some point– that's my motto for life: try everything."

"That's a nice motto," I say, entertained by the concept of creating a motto for your own life.

"Thank you," he laughs, "it's actually inspired by *Dead Poets Society*. As you'll later see, the plot is driven by the concept of 'seizing the day,' so reminding myself to try new things when I can is my version of doing that." He beams with passion.

"That's really nice. I'm excited to see this movie. How did you come up with the idea of making a motto for yourself in the first place?" I encourage him.

"Well, I more so unlocked my motto. I read an article last semester in my business psychology class that said every person has a subconscious internal mantra that they repeat to themselves, sometimes hundreds of times a day, without even knowing it."

"Really?"

"Yes, if you really pay attention, you can learn what you're repeating to yourself– and sometimes what you're saying can be influencing your life more than you know."

"So you listened to your mantra and it was saying 'try everything'?"

"Unfortunately, no. When I listened to my mantra, I realized it was instead saying something a bit negative. But luckily, we learned in my class that you can actually change your mantra."

"So you changed yours?"

"Yep," he tells me with pride, "I thought about what was holding me back and decided to shift my internal monologue to something that would help me overcome those negative thoughts."

"That's very interesting—and impressive that you were able to change your mindset," I remark, intrigued by his drive.

"Yeah, I mean I still catch myself thinking negatively, but that's just a part of life, right? The key is to prevail to a more positive place in those moments," he states.

I tilt up my chin and squint, pensive at the air above my head.

"Do you agree?" he asks, observing my consideration.

"I understand, and I also think it's important to honor and address your negative feelings. Otherwise, they'll follow you, and eventually those feelings will rain down on you like a storm."

I'm immediately mortified at this poetic response. It feels too dramatic for a first date. I stare at my wine with widened eyes.

"That's really interesting; I hadn't thought of looking at it that way," Max says softly.

I bring my gaze back up from my mug, to his face in the glow of the candle. Any indication of judgment is absent from his expression as the warm light engages with his handsome features, bouncing from his eyes to mine, flickering in my chest.

"Just don't forget," he says, "in the moments you face the negativity, you must never lose hope."

That word again. *Hope.* It tickles my heart. He smiles sweetly at me as I stare at him with deep, unconcealable admiration.

"What do you think your motto is?" he asks.

"My motto?" I think about it for a few moments. The words *I can't* burn in my ears. "I'm not sure," I lie, washing away my discouragement with a swig of wine.

"Well, what do you want it to be?" he asked. I had never thought about what I might want in a mantra. I seldom thought about what I wanted in general. At this moment, I thought about what Max had said about choosing a mantra to counteract his negative inner monologue.

"I hope," I say with a little smile. *I hope.*

"I like that," he replies and looks at me with a kind of knowing expression you give someone when you've done something nice for them and feel quite satisfied about it. "Well, *I hope* you like *Dead Poets Society*," he adds.

"Me too."

Max and I talk for another hour by the scarce candlelight about everything. He double majored in Economics and Philosophy in undergrad. He's a dog person. His favorite color is that of the ocean. He'll eat anything that's set in front of him, except for anchovies and blue cheese. He's bad at chess. He's good at poker. He worships no politician. He does worship David Bowie. He started playing piano when he was eight. It's been his dream to be a musician ever since. And although he's making me realize just how much I don't know about myself, we're figuring it out together. Maybe it's the wine, but the awkwardness seems to fade with each minute, and is replaced by an unfamiliar familiarity. Like a smell you recognize but can't remember, or a word that you know but cannot name. Talking to him is like reading a letter in handwriting that's almost yours, but not, or making eye contact with someone through the reflection of a mirror. It feels like even though I've just met him, I have been looking for him in everyone I've ever known.

In fact, by the time we realize we haven't even bothered taking any steps to watch *Dead Poets Society*, it's almost midnight.

"Here, I'll walk you home," Max offers.

"Oh no, that's all right, I'll call a car," I assure him.

"What? No, let me walk you home," he insists.

"Okay." I smile with gratitude, not wanting the night to end.

We take our time promenading down the lamp-lit streets, taking a detour through campus.

"Are you excited for your classes to start?" I ask.

He looks at the ground and presses his lips together, apprehensive. "Maybe not excited, but I suppose I'm anticipatory."

"I can understand not being excited," I admit.

"Really? But you're studying what you like," he remarks.

"And you're not?" I ask.

"Well, I can tolerate business school, but no —it's not my passion," he confirms.

"Yeah, I sort of gathered that it might have something to do with… music?" I joke.

"Indeed."

"So then why are you getting your MBA?" I ask.

"I guess it's my best shot at making decent money."

I nod, considering how lucky I am to not have to think too hard about where my livelihood is coming from.

"Well, you could always try to become a musician after you've saved up some cash," I suggest.

"Yeah," he smiles. But there's something in his eyes that he fights to hide. I know this feeling when I see it. It's mourning. Suddenly, Max seems more real. It makes me want to touch him, to take him in and hold him close. I settle on slipping my hand into his.

When we make it to my apartment, he turns to face me.

"May I kiss you?" he whispers, but he already knows the answer.

I nod slowly.

He wraps his hand around my waist and cups his hand behind my head, and presses his warm lips against mine. When he pulls back, the air feels richer.

"Goodnight," he tells me.

"Goodnight."

I go back up to my unit and decide to make some eggs. I put on some music, turn on the burner under a cast iron pan and throw in some butter and crack an egg over the hot surface. Then I realize I haven't fed Fish yet today.

I walk into my room and go over to his tank and give him a couple of pellets. He's so cute munching up his food.

"My date went well, thank you for asking," I joke with him.

Then I go back to the kitchen to flip my eggs. As I flop the egg onto its back, it sizzles violently, and splatters butter in little fiery speckles across my forearm. I gasp.

"Ow!" I say… *Ow?* It's subtle, but this little shower of stinging– it actually hurts. I stare at my arm confused, as the pain slowly subsides from a panicky fire to a comforting pulse. *That was weird.* The pain felt different– more intense, less enjoyable.

I force myself to forget about it, eat my eggs, and go to bed, unable to stop dreaming about the night.

8.

When I wake up, everything is soft. The light, my sheets, my skin, my hair, everything. Air seems to make it through my nose, down my throat, and into my lungs easier than before—before what, I don't know.

A strong hunger begins growling at me, telling me to get out of bed. But it's not just the usual pinch—it's deeper. I scoot out of bed and get ready quickly, motivated by food. I scour my fridge, but only eggs and hot sauce live there, so I throw on my coat, grab my backpack, and take to the streets.

I locate a little coffee shop down the road from my apartment that I'd passed a hundred times on the way to class and never bothered even considering going into. It's warm inside. I sit in the window with an over-roasted espresso and a lukewarm ham and cheese croissant, perfectly content, watching people hurry by.

Around noon, in the middle of my class, I get a text from Max.

"So when are we going to finish this shitty wine and re-do our attempt at watching Dead Poets Society?"

My heart leaps.

"Tomorrow." I text back almost immediately, bypassing self-control altogether.

I don't hear anything else my professor says.

"He kissed you?" Lillian yells out into the dive bar.

"Yes," I whisper back, "do we need the whole world to know?" I ask, looking around us to see who might've heard, before launching a clumsy dart at the board across from me.

"Sorry, I'm just excited!" She continues to fuss, catapulting her own dart at the board. Neither of us knows how to actually play; we just try to hit the bullseye, and whoever gets the most darts closest to the middle wins. The pin hits the outskirts of the corkboard circle.

"Don't be," I scold her, hypocritically, "I still don't know what he wants from me."

I throw another dart, hitting the ring just before the bullseye.

"I don't know, maybe just to get to know you?" she suggests.

"You're too optimistic," I say.

"You're too unoptimistic," she argues, slightly drunk. "Sometimes, you need to relax and not think so hard about everything that could go wrong," she tells me. Then, while maintaining eye contact with me, she amazingly sinks a dart directly into the bullseye.

"Yes!" she cheers.

I look at her and slump my shoulders, failing to hide a smile of impressed defeat.

"Do you mean 'pessimistic'?" I ask, being a sore opponent as I step up to the throwing line. "And you know that I tend to do better when I think things through," I remind her, carefully throwing my final dart.

Miraculously, it plunges into the board, directly next to Lillian's in the bullseye. Her eyes go wide with disbelief. Then she laughs, scowls, and then rolls her eyes.

"How's Jerrod?" I expertly change the subject.

"What, do you think we *talk* while we're spending all that time together in his bedroom?" she asks. But I know all too well what avoidance looks like to miss Lillian's.

"No need to get defensive," I smile.

"Says *you*!"

"Fine," I say, riding the coattails of my prideful dart victory, "I'll try to be more optimistic," I tell her, as if this hope has not already begun to inspire a change in my attitude.

The next night, I find myself back at Max's house, to watch *Dead Poets Society* as we had planned.

"No Shabbat candles this time?" I tease him.

"No, unfortunately my options for mood lighting tonight were between a book light and a flashlight."

Eventually, after a slightly shorter but equally informative and engaging chat as our first, we take our drinks and conversation to a worn-out leather couch in the living room. I sink into a softened cushion on the far left end of the furniture, and Max plops down a few feet away and sets his wine next to a Chromebook laptop on a low, skinny wooden table that looks like it's survived a global coaster shortage.

"Right then, are you ready for your life to be changed?" he jokes, opening the device.

"I sure am," I say, matching his tone.

"Okay, let's see here…" he says, tapping the account information into the streaming service's homepage.

"Chance Baylor," I read aloud from the username bar, "is that your cinephilic alter ego?"

Max laughs, "I wish; it's actually the name of my brother's husband." He hits *login*. Now I understand the full weight of Henry's homophobic comments.

"With that name, please tell me he's a pop star," I say, concealing my unsolicited pity with humor.

"That's funny you say that, he's actually a songwriter. He's sort of a big deal in New York."

"That's cool, so does your brother live in New York too?"

"Yeah, Oliver ended up there for his residency and got the return offer last year, so he's probably there for the long run."

"He's a doctor?"

"Yep, if you ever need any psychiatric services, I'm sure Doctor Abbott would be happy to help."

These cold words cause my core to contract.

"Psychiatric services?" I confirm.

"Yeah, he's a psychiatrist," he says nonchalantly.

Suddenly, I feel as if I've become transparent. I know there's no logic behind my fears, but I can't help but wonder if somehow he knows about my habits.

"Oh, don't worry, I'm not suggesting you need psychiatric aid," he reassures me with a little joking poke on my shoulder.

I force a laugh and a smile. But my heart sinks. The fact that he's joking almost makes me feel worse. He thinks I *don't* need psychiatric help. What's he going to do when he finds out I probably really *do* need it, more than anyone he knows. I feel the color drain from my face and with it, any hope that Max might ever like me. I am just a consistent upset. *I was so stupid to think this could work,* I think in a panic. I want to scream at Lillian for encouraging me, or Max for inviting me over. Most of all, I want to scream— no, punch at myself for giving into this moronic idea. I want to beat the hope right out of my dumb body. I want to squeeze it from my soul and milk it from my mind and pulverize it so that it might never sneak its way into my thoughts ever again. *I need to get out.*

"Is there a bathroom I could use?" I ask as calmly as possible.

"Yeah, just down the hall, to the left," he points in the direction of the kitchen.

"Thank you." I stand up and head down the hall casually until I'm sure Max is out of sight. Then I pick up my pace, breezing past the bathroom and entering the kitchen. I snatch my coat from the chair I'd placed it on earlier and bank to the right towards a back door. I arrive at my exit and rattle the knob, but it's locked. I frantically fumble in the darkness for a way to unlock it. Suddenly, I hear Max's voice call out from the hallway, "Julia?"

Shit. I run my hands desperately across the door's surface. Miraculously, I find a deadbolt. I flip it, swing open the door, and flee the house. As I stumble around a couple of recycling bins and across the patchy yard, I hear Max's voice again. "Julia!" he shouts, confused. I don't turn around as I catapult through the rusty fence gate into the night.

When I've made it a healthy distance from Max's house, I slow down. Freezing air surfs down my throat and rips at my lungs. Tidings of reality and waves of embarrassment flood my thoughts, which provides little relief to my rising level of anxiety. I was fishing for something I knew I could never pull in. The weight of this realization sits anchored in the depths of my stomach. I'm a wreck. I begin to cry. I sail down the street, salty, back to my home.

When I get back to my apartment, I feel incredibly dirty—filled with ungutted shame. I go to my bathroom and turn on my shower. The pressure of prospective happiness has nearly crushed me. I take off my clothes and step under the stream of hot water and sink to the floor. Then I cast my arm out, aiming it at a scrub brush, and take to washing myself, first relatively gently but thoroughly, brushing my foot and ankle. But I still feel a foul grime under my skin, so I scrub harder, working my way up my calf and thigh, not bothering to ease up on intensity when I reach my burn. Small pearls of blood form across the spots where I've scraped the scabs from the shell of my healing skin. A stinging starts to scratch at a desperate itch that sits in my limbs.

I move to my wrist, swimming the brush back and forth in quick, frantic motions up my arm, until I make it to the place on my shoulder where Max had affectionately prodded me hours prior. I recoil into myself, trying to escape as that nasty feeling seems to latch onto me, digging its barbs down deep into my skin. I panic and scrub harder, up and down, back and forth, until the skin is raw and scaly, bubbling with little blisters and sores. As droplets of water drum against the fresh skin, a pulsing pain binds to the burn and rocks me into a soothing rhythm of soreness. Slowly, the storm in my mind begins to settle.

As I sit on the floor of my shower and reflect, a treasured moment from earlier in the night glitters in my mind. *Just don't forget, in the moments you face negativity, you must never lose hope.* The words bob in my brain, confusing me– for a slippery moment, I actually want to believe them. I almost take the bait, but I catch myself– I reel in my optimism before it gets away from me. I shake my head and finish savoring the rivers of pain floating about my arms and legs. You cannot lose hope if there was never any to begin with.

   After I dry off, I put on a long black robe. Then I sit down at my desk and pull out my notebook from my backpack. I take a pen from my desk drawer and open the book to the torn out page I'd started a poem on a few days back. I read it, and then add to it. I write:

When the day is done and the sun has set
And you're taking in your final breath
And you can't find your heart, there's no beat in your chest
And it's never enough when you're trying your best

Then I pick up my phone and call Henry.

9.

The next morning, as I'm making coffee in my robe, there's a knock on my door. *Lillian's going to freak out when she finds out what's happened*, I think.

"Lil, now is really not a good time!" I yell at the door. A few seconds pass, and I think she might have actually listened for once, but then another round of beats bat against the wood. *Dammit Lillian.* I walk reluctantly across my kitchen to the door.

"I'm sorry, Lil," I unlock the door and swing it open, "I'm just really not in the mood for —" I cut myself off. Standing where Lillian should be is a dark, tall, handsome boy.

"Max?" My voice softens and my face gets warm. I'm humiliated, but somehow feeling simultaneously slightly relieved at the sight of him.

"Julia, hi," he says, guilt in his tone.

"What're you doing here? How did you know what unit was mine?" I motion to my doorstep, too confused to fill in the blanks myself.

"Lillian came by The Coffee Shop this morning for a chai and asked how the night went and I told her how I messed up. She gave me your unit number and told me to come talk to you. I know this is weird, I'm sorry. I was going to give you your space, but then I couldn't stand the thought of you believing I might actually find somebody needing psychiatric help amusing. I had so much fun last night and I just really wanted to say that I'm sorry–"

"Twink?" a dark crunchy voice cackles behind me. Henry follows the laugh into the doorway.

Max's face morphs from a guilty frown into a furious glare.

"What's he doing here?" he wonders aloud.

I freeze, horrified. The reality of my poor choices have come back to screw me.

"Your girlfriend," Henry chuckles.

"Henry." I scold him for his crudity, but it's useless. He turns to me.

"So, Twink here is the reason you haven't been responding to my texts, huh?" Henry scoffs.

I stare at him, begging him with my eyes to stop talking, but he's merciless. He looks back and forth with an open-mouthed grin between Max's upset gaze and my own appalled look.

"Oh, hang on, maybe Twink's also the reason you finally *replied* to my text!"

Since when did he become so insightful? I wonder.

"Henry, just get out," I demand, scooting to the side of the open door.

"I would, but Twink is in my way." Henry gestures to Max, who slowly steps to the side with angry smoke fuming in his eyes.

"Oh my god, stop fucking calling him that." I roll my eyes at his persistent assholeness.

"Well, it's what got you in bed *last* time," Henry says back with a nasty smirk, sliding on his shoes.

"No, it's not," I reply weakly.

"What is he saying?" Max asks, like he already knows the answer.

"What I'm saying is that your little girlfriend here is a whore."

I look down at the ground in disgust with myself. *I deserved that,* I think, stoking the coals of my own burning shame. But a little laugh interrupts my self-loathing.

"I mean, rumor has it," Max says, "you would know." He suddenly sounds offensive. I look up at him.

He's talking to Henry, whose nose has wrinkled in nervous confusion.

"Oh yeah?" Henry asks, doing his best to look unfazed.

"Yeah," Max confirms, "Does the name 'Oliver Abbott' sound familiar to you?"

Henry's face whitens.

"No," he replies much too quickly to be telling the truth.

"Really? Are you sure? He's British, just like me, about the same height too. Played soccer here his sophomore year. Similar features, as he is my brother after all– and he certainly remembers you."

I hold my breath and watch Henry stare at him wide-eyed and reddening. Max takes a step towards him. "Is that maybe why you want me to be gay so badly?" he asks. "Do I remind you of someone from your past?"

Henry lunges with beastly intensity at Max, laying a fat punch on his face.

"Stop!" A scream bursts from my mouth as I try to throw myself between Max and Henry's next punch. But I'm too slow. Instead of following through on his jab, Henry catches me by my arm and tosses me to the side. I feel the back of my body ram into what I know to be my front door. The intensity of Henry's heave sends a gratifying shock through me, and I land on my side on the ground with a floppy thud. I savor the sore pulse for only a moment before remembering Max. I look up just in time to watch him float three succinct, velvety punches across Henry's cheeks. Then, he winds up before Henry can regain his bearings and plants a final uppercut on his dirty mug. Henry falls to a crumpled half-seated, half-laying heap a few feet away from me. Drops of blood fall from his nose like petals and land with little *plops* on the wood flooring.

"Why would you do that to her?" Max yells. I look up to him. He's hot with rage.

From his blood covered lips, Henry spits out two ivory teeth that roll across the ground like dice. Then he laughs. "She probably liked it." He shakes his head in amusement. Disgust digs at me. I hate that he's right.

"Get out!" Max shouts.

Henry obliges, scuffling to his feet and cowering out the door. As soon as he's out of sight, Max rushes down next to me.

"Are you okay?" he asks before sitting back to observe me, like he's checking to see if I've been cracked anywhere during my fall. I follow his eyes as they narrow, and I realize he's caught a glimpse of my blistered leg, which peeks from a section of robe accidentally uncovered during my fall.

"Yeah, I'm fine," I say, quickly pulling the robe back over my leg before looking back up at him. "Oh my god, you're bleeding." I point above his eye.

He raises his hand and touches the spot above his eyebrow; then he winces when his fingers find the cut and pulls them back, dipped in blood.

"I should go," he says.

"No!" I say quickly, not wanting this to be how we leave things– cut up and unrepaired. "I mean, let me at least help you clean that up before you do."

He looks at me for a long second.

"Okay," he agrees.

We both stand up and I close the door before leading the way into my room. I gesture for him to sit on my bed, before I go into my bathroom and turn on the warm water. Then I grab a washcloth from my cabinet and run it under the sink until it's steaming and spongy. When I come back, Max is leaning over, watching Fish dance around his bowl on my dresser. When he sees me, he leaves Fish and comes over to sit on my bed like I'd instructed him to do earlier.

"This might hurt," I warn him before pressing the cloth to his head as gently as possible. My heart stings with guilt as he inhales sharply at the pain. "I'm sorry," I whisper.

"No, I'm sorry," he says, looking down solemnly. "I shouldn't have come here. You clearly wanted to be left alone, and because of me, we both got hurt," he says.

I feel responsible for his confusion and suffering. "It's not you who should be apologizing."

He moves his eyes to mine, waiting for an explanation. I lower the cloth from his head and sit down next to him on the bed.

"Last night, I actually had a wonderful time," I admit, and at this, his eyes light up. "The reason I left wasn't because I was offended. It's because… I was afraid."

His brow furrows into an inquisitive wrinkle.

"What were you afraid of?" he asks gently.

"I was afraid of…" I hesitate, but I feel after the stress I put Max through, I owe him the truth. "myself," I whisper.

"Why?" he asks, sympathy in his eyes.

I'm reluctant to answer the question. I take a deep breath, carefully considering what I'm going to say next. I could lie– make up a reason we can't see each other anymore, but something about his presence makes me feel safe like I've never felt before. In exchange for this, the least I can do is give him my honesty. My stomach seizes. This will certainly bring an end to his admiration of me. But in a way, it's best to get that over with and move on, instead of torturing myself with this idea of a happiness I will never have.

"Because I know that when you learn the truth about what kind of person I am, behind the favorite colors, animals and foods, past the hobbies, hometowns and values, you will not like what you find. And because I really like you," the words *I really like you* effortlessly slip from my lips, "I can't let myself lure you in and then disappoint both of us."

Max looks at me calmly. "You don't know that."

"What?"

"You don't know that I would be disappointed. You would rather sabotage something that has the potential of being good out of the fear that it won't be. You're not afraid of yourself, you're afraid of expectation, of hope. You're afraid of us."

He looks at me intensely, but his tone is kind. I'm taken aback as I consider the reality of his argument. I try to dismiss it.

"You don't understand, it's complicated," I snap, agitated by my inability to get through to him.

"You're right, I don't. I don't understand what could be so complicated that you can't accept that I like you too." A sweet grin sneaks onto his face.

I like you too. He's laid siege to my heart. That's not how this conversation is supposed to go. I don't even deserve his tolerance let alone his approval. I'm trying to sever this connection with Max, not nurture it. That was sure to scare him away and it's failed. I'm cornered. I can only think of one more thing that might get my point across successfully.

I stand up and walk to the center of my room and do something outlandish. I untie my silky robe and let it slip from my shoulders and fall to my feet, displaying myself to Max in only a pair of small pajama shorts and a camisole. Then, slowly, I step forward so that the sun from my bedroom window hits me like a searchlight, exposing every cut, burn, and scar that covers my body.

My cheeks burn. Tears well in my eyes. "How could you like this?" I ask quietly, ashamed of my appearance.

"Did he do this to you?" he asks with a quiet heat on his breath.

I shake my head *no* and watch reality sink into his conscience like a blade.

I retreat back into my robe. Tying the sash back around my waist, I apologize, "I'm sorry I dragged you into this. I–"

"Julia," he interrupts me. I look up at him. As my eyes meet his, a confused panic rushes over me. He's staring at me with what seems like… admiration. I'm baffled.

"You can have scars, and still be worthy of happiness," he tells me calmly.

These wise words rain down like arrows on the mental walls I've built, which shield me from his positivity. What he's said throws me off, weakening me. But as much as I want to give in to his comforting presence and accept his encouraging words, I stand my ground.

"It's more than that. It's more than just cutting or burning or any of it," I say, battling to hold back tears of frustrated humiliation. I'm crumbling. And he looks unconcerned.

In a final effort to counter his undying faith in whatever hope he's found in us, I make a rash decision—I'm going to tell him.

"Max," I plead, sitting next to him on the bed again, "I promise, you do not want this." I have his attention.

I carry myself with a heavy, mourning breath.

"I can't stop hurting myself." *I can't.* "I have an addiction– I am addicted to pain," my meek voice quakes, as I squeeze the words up my throat and out my mouth for the first time ever.

10.

I study Max's face through my tear-blurred vision. Even through compromised eyes, he still appears clearly nonjudgmental, let alone horrified or repulsed. A desperate dismay shoots through my chest. I'm failing to scare him away with the truth. I never anticipated this to be possible. As I reassess my options, slowly, Max leans toward me and delicately lays his cheek on the top of my head. I should rebel against his touch, but I feel so at home surrounded by his embrace. My breath slows. My shoulders relax. I drop my guard and surrender to his affection.

We stay like this for a minute, silent, until Max pulls back his arm, looks at me seriously and speaks.

"Julia, there's something I want you to know."

I look at him. He's hesitant, like he's double checking complex calculations in his head.

"Do you remember how a few nights ago I told you that my inner monologue was saying something negative and I changed it to 'try everything'?" he asks.

"Yes," I reply, trying to predict where he's going with this point.

"Well before, the sentence in question—the one I was repeating to myself—was 'don't do it.' Would you like to know why?"

I nod, unsure whether or not I have the choice to say no, but curious nonetheless. Especially because with this question, he seems to be stalling a confession of some kind.

"Well, you see, I was telling myself, 'Don't do it,' and it was manifesting its way into my every move. But *it* actually all started with something seemingly simple—a small white opium pill."

I freeze. *Max is an addict?* I'm thrown off by this newly discovered concord.

He carries on. "If I told you I was an addict, would that discredit the connection we've been building thus far?"

"Of course not," I answer immediately.

"Well, now that you understand why someone's flaws don't have to define them, I have to tell you that I'm not an addict, nor have I ever been."

I narrow my eyes. *One step ahead of me.*

"But I saw just how easy it was to become one," he continues. "When I was eight, my mom was in a car accident. She broke two ribs and her collarbone. But that was just the beginning of her suffering—taking those painkillers, that was the real accident. I watched her struggle for seven years, in and out of rehabilitation centers. Finally, when my dad filed for divorce and petitioned for full custody of Ollie and me, she got clean and has been sober for the last decade. But she was never a bad person. She had some bad tendencies. Even through the worst of it, she was still so much more than an addict. She taught me to see people for *who* they are to you, not *what* they do to themselves. That's why I would never build a perspective on your character based only on your flaws or let a small part of you overshadow the positive qualities I see."

In this moment, something takes flight from my shoulders. In its wake, a feeling I can only describe as freedom floats around me, like a breeze that flirts with your hair and neck on a sultry summer day. Then, something drops from my chest into my stomach and seems to trickle out from my toes, leaving me in a light, feathery state. From here, a feeling buried deep in my chest starts to bloom, growing with each beat of my heart. It's like what I felt that night on campus, as if the air had suddenly become cleaner. *What is this feeling*, I wonder? I can only describe it as beauty, void of pain. I lock eyes with Max.

He raises a hand to my cheek and wipes away a sneaky tear of relief. Then he holds my head with his hand for a small moment.

Without thinking, I close my eyes and press my lips into his. I taste a sweetness in his mouth and feel a warmth in his breath that, when he pulls away to look at me, leaves me wanting more. I hesitate, noticing his confusion, but selfishly I don't want either of us to use this time for thinking. I move my hand to the back of his neck and coax his face to my own. My tongue finds its way into his mouth, and my hand moves down to grasp the neckline of his shirt. I feel his hand leave my face. Suddenly, a terrible, searing sensation singes through my thigh.

I violently gasp and pull away from the kiss to see that Max has planted his hand on my leg, directly where I burned myself a few days ago, and then scrubbed away the healing skin just last night.

He jumps back, taking away his hand, alarmed.

"What happened?" he asks urgently. "Are you okay?"

"Yeah, I'm okay," I tell myself. But it hurt. It really, truly hurt.

This must be pain without beauty, I think. I look helplessly at Max as I bounce between a subtle joy at this progress and a horrific confusion at this new feeling. I breathe the only words I can think to describe my state.

"I'm scared," I say. But this feeling quickly morphs into guilt. Thanks to my fear-inspired actions, I've betrayed the one person in this world who might understand my disposition—the one person who might be able to help me fight my addiction.

"I'm so sorry."

"It's okay," he gives me a comforting nod, "I know what it's like to be afraid. I used to be so scared that I might try the wrong thing at the wrong time, and that made me terrified to try anything. But I learned to surrender this caution and turn to hope instead of giving in to fear."

"How do I learn to do that?" I demand.

"The only way there is, is through persistence, and this will take some time," he admits.

I sit in silence for a few moments, pondering what to do next, until I settle on doing nothing at all and sit in silence for a few more.

"I think we could both use some time to process this, given everything that happened last night" he says softly.

"You're right, I'm sorry," I nod in agreement, immeasurably guilty for my actions. "In the meantime, let's be friends?" I suggest. My words are soaked in desperation. I can't lose him altogether.

"Friends." He nods understandingly, but I sense a twang of disappointment in his reaction. "I have to go back to The Shop soon; I'm on my break, but I have something for you before I go."

He reaches his hand behind him, into his back pocket, and brings it back holding a little book, which I hadn't noticed he'd been carrying.

"I figured reading was maybe more your thing," he smiles and extends a copy of *Dead Poets Society* to me.

"Thank you," I say. As I move to take the book from his hand, I catch a glimpse of his tarnished watch. "Oh my gosh, is that time accurate?"

"Indeed."

I jump up from the bed. "I'm late for class," I say on my way to my dresser, "and if I miss any more, my professor will probably fail me. I'm so sorry, but I have to get dressed," I turn to him, clutching some indistinguishable garments, "can you show yourself out?"

"Yeah, not a problem," he agrees politely and holds up the book, "I'll leave this on your desk."

"Okay," I say, turning toward my bathroom, but then spinning back to him, "Oh, and Max, thank you for the book, and especially for coming here," I tell him.

"I'll see you later," he smiles.

I duck into the bathroom and close the door and get dressed and ready as quickly as I can. Then I run over to my desk and I sweep the contents off its surface into my bag, swish my pill down my throat with a swig of cold coffee and swing open my apartment door, throwing myself in the direction of campus.

As I arrive at class, kids are gathered around Professor Bowling's podium, shoveling sheets of poetry into a messy pile before him. I pull out my notebook, which I remember stashing my poem in the night before, but it's nowhere to be found. It must have fallen out from its place between the pages in my rush to get to campus. I give up my search and sit down without turning in an assignment.

"Okay, class, get yourselves situated, because today, we're going to prime our poetic perspectives for our next poet, Emily Dickinson, and dive into the depths of her captivatingly imaginative works!" Professor Bowling broadcasts across the classroom with a smile.

This time he has a PowerPoint, which was no doubt created by a teacher's assistant, as this tool is far too advanced to be the product of Bowling's limited technological abilities. He clicks a button on an ancient boxy remote, which remarkably triggers the screen to successfully change slides, from the title page to a black and white image of Dickinson. Professor Bowling is just as shocked at his technological success as the rest of the class.

"Well, isn't that neat?" he remarks, before carrying on with his lecture. "Emily Dickinson was born in Amherst, Massachusetts, in 1830, and published no work during her lifetime. Her sister, however, served as the main catalyst to her immortal fame. After Emily's death in 1886, her sister, Lavinia, discovered over two-thousand poems and letters stashed away in Emily's room in a large chest. Why didn't Emily publish them herself?" Bowling looks at us with a brow raised, feeding into our wispy anticipation, "Well, for the last twenty-five years or so of Emily's life, she was said to never leave her house, becoming one of history's most famous recluses," Bowling reveals.

"Why didn't she leave her house? Was she, like, depressed?" Matt, the football player, blurts out.

"It's possible," Bowling humors Matt's simple theory, "but more specifically, it was theorized that she suffered from extreme agoraphobia—a fear of public mishappenings, sometimes categorized as a social anxiety disorder."

Matt stares at him with his mouth half open, likely failing to comprehend how what Bowling described is any different from depression. Bowling moves on.

"This reclusive nature is on brand with Dickinson's self-depriving habits, having never pursued fame, married, or moved away from her home. Speculations as to why she exhibited this behavior are best showcased, in my opinion, in one of her poems."

Bowling clicks his remote, and a poem greets us from the screen. It reads:

> *Success is counted sweetest*
> *By those who ne'er succeed.*
> *To comprehend nectar,*
> *Requires the sorest need.*

After a few moments, Bowling asks, "Does anyone want to take a guess as to what Dickinson meant in this stanza?"

I'm surprised as my hand pulls itself into the air above me.

"Yes, Ms. Wright?"

"I think what Dickinson was trying to say is that the thought of love, success and happiness is more fulfilling than the actual labor and risk associated with pursuing it."

"Precisely my interpretation," Bowling emphasizes, "and she did exactly that. Instead of risking failure or labor, she squandered her goals and ended exactly where she started. Maybe she was satisfied, but personally, it's not what I would define as 'happiness' for myself. That being said, her poetry was groundbreaking, so let's dive into that, shall we?"

As I drift in and out of the lecture, I remember that I'm stuck– between the beautiful safety of pain and the painful reality of beauty, which

I think may be the makings of love. I'm terrified. I'm inspired.

Part 3

11.

“So, why exactly did you think it was a good idea to give a stranger my exact address after I literally ran away from our date?” I confront Lillian as we walk from her class to her apartment.

“Okay, I know how it looks, but you should’ve heard the way he was talking about you! The man is head over heels! And I figured if you could work things out with Henry after you literally slapped him, maybe you could give Max a second chance,” she confesses.

"Okay, I know you just want the best for me, but that wasn't your place, and as I explained earlier, it got a lot of people hurt." I admonish her softly.

"I know, I'm sorry. Did you at least smooth things over?" She snoops as we enter her building.

"I guess you could say that," I reply, climbing away from her up the stairs to her floor.

"Well, what happened?" She calls up to me.

"We agreed to be friends," I call back down to her from her doorway.

"Friends, huh?" she huffs.

"Yeah, it just felt like things were moving a little fast."

"I'll say! Jesus, that or I'm out of shape!" she jokes, joining me at her unit, out of breath and opening the door to a fuzzy gray cat with white paws, curiously perched on her dining room table.

"Bean! How many times have I told you? Off the table!" she yells.

He just stares at her tauntingly. She rolls her eyes, throws down her bag, and strides over to the table to scoop him up.

"Ugh, you stink!" She turns her crinkled face away from him as she sets him down on a fuzzy pink carpet at the base of a cherry red, lip-shaped velvet couch.

I follow her in and close the door behind me.

Every time I come into Lillian's apartment, I swear she's redecorated, or at least added to the existing maximalist display of color, art, and gadgets. Some call it hoarding, but she calls it collecting. I do a quick scan of the place to see if I can pick out any new additions. Her modern vaginal-esque painting still hangs above her lip couch. But on a quirky black table, which I can only describe as having cow udders, sits an ashtray shaped like a mermaid who looks like she's about to climax. *Bingo.*

"Love the mermaid," I fib, "is it new?"

"Yes! I know, right? It's so camp," she says, opening her fridge. "God, I'm starving. Do you want anything?"

"I'm okay on food, but I'll take an espresso."

"Help yourself!" She gestures to a coffee machine.

"Thanks." I go set my backpack down by the dining table and move to the kitchen counter to make my drink. I grab a turquoise espresso cup out from the cabinet above me and place it below the machine, then pop in a coffee pod. Right as I punch the *brew* button, my phone vibrates in my back pocket. I pull out the device to see who's calling me. The caller ID reads *Jacqueline Levin*, a name which rarely shows itself to me these days.

Jackie Levin is quite a despicable character, in my opinion. She's not a good person. Rather than naming the things she is not good at, it would be quicker to name the things she is. That list begins with the word *day* and ends with *drinking*. Completing a list of what she's bad at is much more difficult, but one can try. She's bad at marriage, or at least picking a husband, having been remarried twice before the age of forty. She's not great at saving money, which is probably why she married for it. She's lousy at remembering birthdays. She's awful at thinking about things other than herself. She's terrible at making friends and worse at keeping them. She's horrendous at small talk. That's why when she does call you, you'd better pick up, because it's likely important— she is not calling for the pleasantries of conversation.

I turn to Lillian, who's layering pickles on a bed of jam spread over a piece of raw white bread. "I'd better take this." I tell her, and head for her bathroom. I close the door and slide open the phone's *answer* icon.

"Hi, Mom," I say.

"Hello honey! How are you doing? Are you doing well?" she asks in a rushed voice.

"Yeah, I suppose–"

"Oh good, honey, really, that's good to hear. Good things all around. You see, I'm calling to let you know that David and I are taking the twins to–"

"Mom, Hanna and Isaac aren't twins," I blurt.

"Oh, well I know that, but doesn't saying 'the twins' just sound so nice? Anyway, we're all taking a trip to Mexico over the holiday break and we'd love for you to join us."

"Maybe," I say, even though taking a trip anywhere with Jackie sounds like a trip to hell. "When are you going?"

"In a few weeks, on the 25th."

"Of December?" I clarify.

"Yes, honey, I know it's Christmas, but David said those were the only flights left, and we can always celebrate once we get there."

"Okay. I'll think about it," I lie.

"Oh, marvelous honey, really. Listen, I've got to run, but I love you and I'm so glad you're doing good."

"Okay, bye, mom–" I'm cut off by a series of beeps which signal the end of our call. I exit the bathroom to Lillian eating her pickle jam and turkey sandwich.

"How was that?" she asks with her mouth full.

"Good, Jackie's flying to Mexico on Christmas, so I don't have to see her," I say, walking over to the kitchen to grab my espresso.

"Well, shit, looks like you're all freed up to join me in New York!" she exclaims.

"I guess I am," I consider, "but I don't want to do that to your mom."

"What? Are you kidding? It's not like you're some stranger, you're practically family, she'd love to have you! Here, I'll text her right now."

"Okay, you can text her, but if she shows even the slightest hint of apprehension–"

"Julia, stop that."

"What?"

"Stop selling yourself short. People like to have you around. I know your mom might not make you feel that way, and it can be easy to doubt yourself, but you have to just trust me. You don't need to run from people when they try to show you love," she says.

I fail to hide my surprise at her sudden passionate sermon of aggressive wisdom.

"I'm sorry, that was uncalled for," she apologizes. "I think I'm about to get my period or something, and I just needed to be dramatic for a second."

"That's okay," I laugh it off.

Then I raise my cup to my lips and sip my espresso. Maybe it's the unfamiliarity of a foreign machine, but today, the coffee tastes almost unbearably strong. I chalk it up to low quality beans, and try not to make a fuss about it. The last thing I need is to get all particular about my coffee.

I try to do homework on Lillian's lip couch for about an hour, but I can't take myself seriously sitting there under a vagina painting, staring at a ceramic orgasming mermaid, so I pack up and head to the library. There, I'm actually able to focus, motivated by the promise of beginning *Dead Poets Society*.

When I get my work done, I want to start reading, but something stops me. I'm not sure what it is, but getting the book out, there in the library, and reading it in the open feels rampantly violating, like the feeling you might get when you don't want someone you just met to watch you eat something messy. I want to be able to savor this book that Max gave me, and in order to properly do that, I feel like I need to be in privacy.

I walk to the safety of my home, where I feel comfortable enough to liberate the book from my backpack. I lay down on my couch and crack it open to its first page and begin inhaling the words from the paper. I find myself searching the lines for clues as to why Max is how he is. *How did he learn to choose hope over fear?* I wonder.

I make it to page nineteen before I notice something curious while absorbing a passage about one of the main characters, Neil, who pricks his finger with a pin in front of his roommate, Todd—

Todd winced, but Neil just stared at the blood intently. It's an out-of-place line, the first in violent nature in the story thus far. Reading it has made me realize that as I've been so fixated on finding answers, I have not once attempted to cut my fingers with the pages as I've progressed.

In a moment, inspired more so by curiosity rather than bravery, I make the decision to conduct an experiment. I single out a page and extend my index finger so that it makes contact with the sheet at just the right angle. Then I pull my finger down, producing a miniature incision across the tip, as I've done a thousand times before. A venomous sting rushes into the slit and pulses through my hand. Normally satisfying, this sensation is far from it. As hypothesized, the pain is variably unpleasant. I watch, confused, as a drop of blood glides down my finger. I'm overwhelmed with a diverse platter of emotions. For a moment, I feel fear. I try to imagine how I will cope with this new terrible pain as a replacement for my comfort in discomfort, but panic outweighs any prayer of finding a rational solution.

Tears drip from my eyes in tandem with blood from the gash. Then, a moment later, I realize that alongside this fear, I feel something else—I feel free. No fear can bind me. No pain can ground me. Nothing can hold me down. I think of Sylvia Plath's phoenix, rising from the ashes. Not even fire can stop me. *This is it*, I think. *Hope.*

I finish the rest of *Dead Poets Society* in that same sitting. Then, I feel profoundly hungry, so I make myself a peanut butter banana sandwich, eat that, and then hop in bed and read the book again.

Although the story was enjoyable the first time, I don't read it a second time out of love for the plot. I do it because Max said it was one of his favorites, and as I'm reading it, I like the feeling of reading something he gave me. I fall asleep with it in my hand like an idiot.

12.

For the next few days, everything I do reminds me of him. I read poetry and I imagine he's written it. I write poetry like he might read it. I eat, sleep and exist like he's watching me. I dream up delusion after delusion over what he'd think about everything I do and what he'd do about it. I picture him with me, doing the things too. How his hands would hold something, how his eyes might track and trace my face, body and surroundings. When I catch myself doing it I get mad at myself and then imagine what Max would do about that too. I want him there with me, but I'm too afraid. I haven't even visited The Coffee Shop since our falling out. Lillian had called it a "slowing down", but I'm not convinced.

An over-sized spongy crimson hand waves dangerously close to my nose, breaking me from my obsession. I direct my attention to the field, passionately uninvested in either team's progress. Lillian has managed to drag me to the school's final football game of the season. And I've managed not to let anyone spill their water bottles, full of everything but water, on me. So far, the only thing I've learned about football is that it's an excuse for boys to engage in rough foreplay, before piling up atop each other, completely liberated from the clutches of societal heterosexual expectation.

Just then, a roar of pride runs through the bleachers across the field from where Lillian and I are seated. The blue team has scored another touchdown. The quarterback responsible prances back and forth at the end of the field like a little bird performing a mating dance, while his teammates flap and squawk about in support of his victory.

"Boooooo!" someone above me in the bleachers chants.

I look up to a skinny blonde dude with a perv-stache pumping his fist in the air with disapproval, like he believes that if he does it hard enough the referee might cancel the points and crown our team the winners. His friends join in on the heroic, certainly impactful and undoubtedly productive *booing*, bouncing around, joggling the bleachers in protest. *I'm too old to be here*, I think. Or maybe just too mature.

As I turn around, I feel their cold, wet anger douse me in the form of Everclear. Despite basic physics and logic, one of the bozos sprayed their drink towards the field, which sits at least twenty feet away from our position in the stands. We can barely see the players last names, hence why the drink landed on my head and shoulders instead of anywhere near the referee or team.

"Hey, what the fuck, man!" Lillian bursts out, wiping sweet vodka from her cheeks and flicking it back at the boys.

"Oh shit," one of the boys murmurs, clearly sloshed, "Sorry 'bout that!"

"Uhg!" Lillian scoffs, realizing fighting with these drunks will do nothing.

"Does this mean we can leave?" I ask.

"Yeah," she sighs with disappointment. Empathy tugs at my sleeve.

"How about we go warm up at that pub on Mt. Auburn?" I suggest.

Lillian's face lights up. "Okay," she smiles.

We walk over to the pub, freezing, and grab a table, which is good, because thirty minutes later, the place is packed with disappointed football fans. I've never seen people celebrate as hard as they mourn.

"Hey, there's Jerrod," Lillian laughs pointing towards the door. Sure enough, I spy Jerrod coming into the bar with a group of his friends, all dressed up in dark red sports fan clothing.

"Oh my god," Lillian grabs me, "and Max!" She exclaims. My stomach doubles.

"Shhh!" I shush her urgently, feeling my cheeks turn the same shade of red as our football team's jersey.

Jerrod spots Lillian, who, to my dismay, doesn't seem to ever blend in, and the boys start across the bar to our table. I look down, trying to compose myself but it feels useless. I'm just going to have to deal with the embarrassment of him knowing the truth about my addiction. I feel ill. He probably won't even want to talk to me–

"Hey Julia," Max says.

His voice interrupts my panicked embarrassment. I look up to his calm, handsome face. *One step ahead of me.*

"Hi," I say, my voice noticeably shaking.

"Are you okay?" He asks softly.

"Yeah," Lillian interrupts, coming to my rescue, "we're just cold. We got drenched in Everclear by some idiots at the game," she says, forcing a little shiver herself.

"I'm sorry about that," Max says, taking off his jean jacket and draping it on my shoulders. My heartbeat quickens as I smell sandalwood and feel his residual body heat wrap around me with the jacket.

"Thank you," I say shyly.

"Mind if we join you?" Jerrod asks, sliding into the booth and wrapping his arm around Lillian.

"Sure, go right ahead," Lillian says sarcastically.

"Thanks," Max smiles, sitting next to me, across from Lillian and Jerrod.

"I didn't see you at the game; where were you sitting?" Jerrod asks.

"Smack in the middle," Lillian tells him.

"Ah, we were up and to the left," Max says.

"You guys went together?" Lillian asks, a little delight in her voice.

"Yeah, my roommate went too and we all met up there," Max explains, gesturing to his roommate, who is now sitting at the bar with some other people, putting back beers like there's a drought.

"I have a feeling that's not the last time he'll be seeing those beers," Max whispers to me, also looking at his roommate.

I breathe a laugh.

"Where were you this week? I didn't see you at The Shop," he asks.

His concern is encouraging, but my answer is demeaning. I look over to Lillian for conversational support, but she's been rendered useless as she's begun making out with Jerrod, who's probably too drunk to remember he's in public. Lillian is probably just too proud to care.

"I'm not sure," my eyes dart down from Lillian to my hands in my lap. "I guess I figured it would be better to give you some space," I admit.

"We agreed to be friends, not enemies. You're welcome at the shop whenever you please," he tells me.

"I was also embarrassed," I confess.

"Because of… Henry?" he asks.

"That's a big part of it," I nod, then look up to him, "and not only what I did do, but also because of what I haven't done," I say quietly.

"What do you mean?" he asks, leaning in closer. I look back at Lillian and Jerrod locking tongues.

"Let's get a drink," I nod to the bar. Max dips his chin in approval and slides from the booth and we go over to a corner at the bar.

"You were saying…" he encourages me.

I sigh, "You seize every day, tackling your fears head-on," I look at him with defeat, "and I just run from mine."

"You said before you were afraid of yourself; now you're afraid of me too?" he jokes.

"No," I counter, "but you do make me aware. It's like every time I talk to you, I'm reminded of what I can't be," I reveal.

He looks at me with cool revelation and I notice the cut on his eyebrow is starting to look a little better.

"What makes you think I don't feel the same way about you?" He asks. I'm taken aback.

"I don't know," I say hiding my shock with sarcasm, "maybe it has something to do with the fact that you're a hot, philosophical musician who just happens to be smart enough to get an MBA even though he doesn't really want to, and I'm just a girl who told you about her weird addiction."

"I'm not reducing you to that," he says, sounding upset, "why are you doing it to yourself?"

I open my mouth but no words come out.

"You haven't even considered that I might be thinking the same thing about myself– That a beautiful, empathetic and intelligent poet has no business being interested in an unpassionate business student who lacks direction," he says matter of factly.

"That's not–"

"What? Not what you think about me? Well it's all about perspective. And until you can get some perspective on who you are, separate from your addiction, you're not going to be able to accept the truth about how the people that care about you see you."

"Why do you care about me?" I look at him, confused.

"I don't know," he shakes his head, looking away defeated, but then turning back to me, "Maybe you remind me of someone I love."

I nod, pausing, before speaking.

"I know the feeling."

"We can stick with the friend thing for now, but don't avoid me either," he moves my hair from my face so that he can look directly in my eyes, "I like seeing you."

My heart shakes.

We go back to the table, where Jerrod and Lillian have come up from their makeout session for air, and I try my best to act unsuspiciously normal. But hope creeps up my arms and legs and burns holes in my skin where I scrubbed myself raw. It's the same, different hurt. Like the throbbing is more colorful, but in a way that's overwhelming, overstimulating. In a way that I want it to stop. But still I'm fascinated. This is real pain.

For the next two weeks, on and off, I continue to feel pain differently. It's stressfully unpredictable. I take a hot shower and enjoy the burn. I accidentally cut myself shaving and dislike the nip. I brush knots from my hair and appreciate the subtle pull. I cut my nails too short and despise the bite. I touch my toes and take pleasure in the stretch. A headache finds me and I'm aggravated by the pressure. I'm thrown by just how much pain I hadn't clocked in my everyday life. I mourn both the comfort in pain, and the time and energy lost turning to it. This newfound awareness is thrillingly draining. A handful of times, I feel a tingling craving, but I'm quickly reminded of my new reality if I so much as threaten to fulfill these urges. I feel suspended in my new outlook. As I float away from everything I've known to be true, I fly, grasping at thin air for a new reality. But I fly nonetheless, as I'm slowly learning to replace *I can't* with *I hope*. The only thing that doesn't feel sporadic about my life is my flirtatious friendship with Max. My daily visits to The Coffee Shop are what ground me. I look forward to seeing Max all day before I go, and think about him almost all day after. He is my hope.

Today is no different.

"Hey, Julia, happy Friday!" Max says cheerfully as I bounce up to the register.

"Hey," I smile. Butterflies still flutter around in my stomach each time I see him.

"The usual?" he asks.

"I think I'm actually going to try something new today," I tell him.

"Hey, you know how I feel about trying new things," he jokes. "What will it be then?"

"May I have a cappuccino, please?"

"Absolutely, one cappuccino coming right up," he says, writing my name on a large cup.

I pay and scoot over to the pick-up counter.

"Are you excited for winter break?" I ask. I'm becoming quicker at filling silences.

"I am, I'm going back to London for a week to visit my family. I'm flying out tomorrow, actually," he tells me happily as he starts up the espresso machine.

"That'll be nice," I say, watching him froth the milk.

"Indeed. What are your plans?" he asks.

"I finished my last final yesterday, so I'm taking the train to New York tonight with Lillian," I tell him, feeling no need to specify that I'll be there through Christmas.

"Oh, that should be fun. How's she feeling, by the way?" he asks. Lillian has been sick with some stomach flu for the last week or so.

"She's doing all right. I'm actually just coming from hers now. I brought her some soup and crackers. She seems to be on the mend," I report.

"Good to hear; hopefully, she'll be back to one hundred percent by Christmas!" he says, handing me the now full cup. "A cappuccino for you, m'lady."

"Thank you," I giggle stupidly. "Well, I'd better get going. I can't stay for your break today, sadly. I have to pack," I remind him.

"That's all right. Here, before you go, I wanted to give you something," he says, hurrying around the counter with his hand in his pocket. I look at him with inquisitive admiration. He hesitates awkwardly and then extends both his arms out. "Safe travels; I'll see you soon," he says and wraps himself around me in a warm hug.

I blush. "Yeah, see you soon," I say timidly.

"You too are cute," a raspy voice, close in proximity, observes. I pull away from Max and see his manager, Gina, leaning forward on the counter with her elbow and her head in the palm of her hand, admiring us.

I ignored her comment but responded with a warm smile and a "Merry Christmas, Gina. See you in a few weeks."

On my way out, I overhear her talking to the employees.

"All right, I've got a Christmas gift for you people after all—there's a big winter storm coming up the coast, and we're locking up early!"

Back at home now, I begin to prepare for my departure. I say an objectively unnecessarily sentimental goodbye to the cluelessly excited Fish and drop him off at my neighbor's place. Then I do some dishes, make my bed, and start packing items into my backpack.

When I pull out my purse, I feel a heavy object resting dormant and forgotten at its bottom. I put my hands in the pouch and retrieve something cold. It's the letter opener that I accidentally stole from Jerrod's family study the night I met Max. I look at it closely, trying to recall why I ever felt compelled to bring the tool's tip to my skin. I see that the point is still crusted in the deep crimson brown of my dried blood.

I bring it to my bathroom, where I carefully wash and dry it, and set it aside on my dresser shelf, where I'll remember to restore it to the Kaminkis' brownstone in one way or another upon my return to Boston.

On the train to New York, Lillian spends a good chunk of the ride in the bathroom, so I'm forced to spend time with my thoughts. I stare out the window, watching fields of frozen, long-ago plowed crops pass by. A thought plants itself in my mind. Although Max has been consistently flirting with me the last couple weeks, he hasn't once brought up the topic of pursuing more than a friendship with me. This seems peculiar, given that just a few weeks ago, he was so adamant that I was special to him. Just then, Lillian comes back from the bathroom.

"Hey," I say, "how are you doing, there?"

"Oh, I'm alright; it's probably just a combination of whatever flu I've had with the train's motion."

"Yeah, that's probably it." I agree.

"What're you up to?" she asks, glowing with fever.

"Just thinking," I say, not wanting to worry her.

"About?" she presses.

"Oh nothing." I force the corners of my mouth upward, but she knows me better than that.

"Common, spit it out. It'll help me take my mind off what *I've* been spitting out!" she jokes.

I give in, "I just feel like Max is losing interest in me," I confess.

"What makes you say that?" she asks.

"I just don't feel like things are going anywhere," I admit.

"Hang on, who friend-zoned whom?" she clarifies.

"He friend-zoned me," I tell her.

"Okay, but did he do it because he wanted to be only friends, or did he do it because you were both scared?"

"Probably the latter," I say.

"So there's your problem!" She motions above us with her hands, as if the solution to my dilemma is written somewhere in the air. "What will you do about it?" she asks, as if it's obvious.

"Well, now he's leaving for a break. There's nothing I can do about it right now, so I guess I'll just try to stop thinking about it and hope he comes around," I respond.

"BZZT! Wrong!" She yells, mimicking a game show buzzer. "Call him or text him! You can't just sit around hoping for something to happen! If you want something, get up and go get it!"

"What? I don't want to bother him. Plus I'm fairly certain he's moving on and so should I."

I don't tell her the full truth– I'm worried that maybe the reality of my situation has finally gotten to him. That the weight of my addiction has pushed him away. That I need him to prove to me again that he wants me, even if it's not fair to keep making him demonstrate his interest in me.

"Well—" She freezes, turning white. "You know what, I'll be right back," she says, then clutches her mouth and runs back to her unofficial seat assignment in the bathroom, on the floor next to the toilet.

13.

When we make it to Grand Central Station, large, fluffy snow clumps have already begun to pour from the sky, coating the gritty streets of New York City in a layer of white. The flakes reflect and illuminate the already awesome display of lights, flickering on one by one as the sun falls, long before the people of the city are ready to surrender to the darkness of night.

"You said East 83rd and Park Ave?" The driver confirms after turning down his radio from the front seat of the taxi.

"That's correct," Lillian replies.

He nods and turns the weather station back up to a staticky reporter's voice, squawking, "Folks, the snow is coming down hard and showing no sign of letting up!"

"No shit, Sherlock!" the driver yells back at the radio.

I'm glad we took a cab. We could have ridden the subway from Grand Central, but Lillian said she wanted us to be able to savor the city in the snow. "You never know if it's going to stick," she'd said, "let's appreciate it while we can." I also know for a fact that she hates the subway with a rotten passion and probably wouldn't have been able to endure its putrid smell in her sickened state. But if I'm being honest, this cab's smell isn't much of an upgrade, so I'd better at least make the most of the view. I watch as the buildings, cars, and even the people are slowly enveloped in the thick fog of cold crystallized bliss.

There's something about the first snow of the season that brings a little bit of chaos and a monumental amount of joy to the place it touches. Through the clouds of snow, I spot Christmas tree stands selling spruces dressed up in ornaments. Kids build snowmen and barrel fistfuls of blizzard at each other from behind their bodega fruit-stand strongholds. Apartment porch railings are strung with multicolored holiday lights. Pristinely wrapped presents, oversized candy canes, glittering menorahs, and intricate hanging paper snowflakes display themselves in shiny shop windows.

After twenty-five minutes or so, the taxi comes to a halt in front of an elegant Romanesque-looking building. Lillian pays, and we exit the vehicle, dash through the winter wonderland, and enter the lobby of her complex.

I've only been here once before, on a long weekend last year, but even in such a short amount of time, the glamor of Lillian's New York lifestyle was made well apparent. Seemingly, nothing has changed since then. The doorman calls a porter, who helps Lillian bring her overstuffed duffle bag up to the penthouse. Lillian then shows me to the larger of the two guest rooms.

After I get ready for bed, I turn off my lights. I keep my curtains open—I like how the city keeps me company. At this moment, I can't imagine ever wanting to vacation anywhere else. Mr. and Mrs. Gasper can. They're in Cappadocia until the morning of the 24th. But unlike Jerrod, we have no parties planned tonight, or any night during the next week, in the advent of their parental hiatus—and thank goodness because tonight we're both exhausted for our respective reasons. I climb into a king-sized bed fitted with what feels like one billion thread-count sheets, lay my heavy head on a feather-filled pillow, and imagine what it would be like for Max to be there, lying next to me. It makes me sad. I close my eyes to the comfort of my dream, manufactured by my desire.

The next morning, sunbeams nudge me awake from the same position in which I fell asleep. A few minutes later, Lillian comes bursting through the door to my room.

"Rise and shine, Sleeping Beauty! We've got a whole day of New Yorking ahead of us!" she announces.

"Someone's feeling better," I laugh.

We start the day with a coffee, not too far from Lillian's penthouse, and work our way down from the Upper East Side, eventually making it to Flatiron, where Lillian shows me her second favorite dog park (she's never before had a dog) and we grab pizza and gelato from Eataly. Then, we go back up to Rockefeller Center, gawk at the tree, watch the ice skaters and window shop around the outskirts of Bergdorfs. Afterwards we take a cab back to her apartment so we can get ready for dinner.

If there was ever a "New York uniform" prescribing all black clothing to this city, Lillian must've missed the memo. She comes down the stairs from the second floor wearing silver jeans, bright purple heels and a green sweater with a printed yellow needle that's made to look like it's halfway through stringing her a necklace of actual pearls, which have been sewn into the garment. She carries a red plaid purse.

"I missed my clothes that I couldn't fit in my Cambridge closet!" She exclaims, hugging the purse. She's curled her blonde and pink locks so that they hang in shining ringlets across her shoulders. Suddenly she gasps.

"Oh my god, Julia, you look stunning!" She compliments me.

I look down timidly at my stocking-covered legs standing in my petite black heels. "Thank you, so do you," I say, hiding myself in my long-sleeve navy v-neck minidress behind my black clutch. I had more time to do my makeup than usual while Lillian was busy reuniting with her wardrobe.

After dinner on the Upper East Side, Lillian suggests we go to a piano bar a few blocks away. The snow hasn't melted much, and I'm pretty tired, but she's convincing, so I agree to go. We trudge down the sidewalk until we enter through an unassuming backdoor entrance and navigate a cold concrete hallway to where a second door awaits us at the end.

Through this door is what I can only describe as a prohibition-style paradise.

A slow burn of jazz music emanates from a band playing on a platform stage at the center of the room. Small round tables host candles, whose flames fan the allure of the atmosphere as they sway in the darkness. Desire dances in the eyes of those exchanging glances. Glasses are clinked, swapped, and emptied. Whispers bounce from lips and flit their way to ears. Second-hand cigarette smoke sneaks into noses. Shadows imitating amorous bodies project the promises of later romance across the walls.

Lillian and I are seated at the bar, where she orders a ginger ale and I grab a glass of cabernet. I still don't know how to appreciate wine, but at least I no longer reject its enjoyable intricate flavors. We sit there, chatting in between appreciating the music, until the band announces a brief intermission. The piano player, an older gentleman in a tuxedo and a red bowtie, joins us at the bar. He winks at Lillian.

"Silver fox?" I whisper to her. Normally she might come up with a quick quip back, or joke along with me, but she just looks at me, grinning softly like she knows something I don't. I look at her deeply trying to read her mind.

Suddenly, behind us, I hear a drizzle of notes leak from the piano in a vaguely familiar pattern. I lean around Lillian, whose arcane smile has grown wider. The pianist still sits in his spot, nursing a drink. *If he's not playing, then who is?*

The melody plays in my ears like a memory. *Could it be?* I slowly turn my head, directing my gaze to the center of the room. My stomach drops.

There, sitting at the piano is, of all people, Max.

Questions overwhelm me. What is he doing here, in New York, at the same piano bar as Lillian and me? Did he lie to me about what he was doing over break? Did he not want to see me, so he said that he was leaving the country? Flustered and panicked, I scoot away from my bar chair, stand up, and start off toward the exit. But something stops me in my tracks.

It's the vibrations of a voice. A passionate, clear, heartfelt singing voice that grabs onto me and holds me tight and won't let me leave. It sings:

When the day is done and the sun has set
And you're taking in your final breath
And you can't find your heart; there's no beat in your chest
And it's never enough when you're trying your best

When you're all out of hope and you're chasing the dawn
And you've emptied your glass, and you're three sails gone
When you're feeling so weak and they tell you "be strong"

He did it. He's the one who stole my poetry. My face blazes with furious embarrassment. How dare he take something that, as far as he knew, was meant for only my eyes, and broadcast it about this room like it's his prize? How dare he publish my feelings, sing them as if he understands them, as if they are his own. I'm about to throw open the door when I hear that the last line has been changed. His voice rings out:

It suddenly comes to me what I've missed in my presumptuous panic. I drop my guard and into my heart flows an emotional realization. This is not plagiarism. This is a profession. I turn back around. He continues to sing:

> *We've all done some things that don't make us proud*
> *And we've all seen some things that we can't say out loud*
> *Even if you can't feel your heartbeat, it's still there*
> *Maybe you just need someone to remind you where*
>
> *And we all must fall so let us first fly*
> *I will follow you until the day that I die*
> *So, since our lives are short, we only have so long*
> *I'm asking you to be my swan song*

He continues to play. Then, suddenly, the violinist lights up their strings. The bass cello joins in, and a glorious symphony of colorful notes float from the instruments like smoke, accumulating in the air like a masterpiece. The song teeters between tragic and triumphant. It heats up, then cools down, freezes over, and then melts.

When the notes start to boil back up again, something wells in my heart and falls from my eyes. I finally understand what Max was describing back in study. *They see the beauty in life and in death, even if there is pain present, and this is a lot to feel at once,* he'd theorized, referring to the question of why people cry to music. I want to cling to this feeling forever. This understanding that beauty does not need to be pain, but can exist alongside it. But like all things, it's temporary. As the song ends, so does my enlightenment, but it's left me feeling better. It has left me filled with hope.

As he stands up from the piano, I find my feet floating my body towards him. I forget everything– my prior anger and confusion, the people around us, and even my doubts are left behind by my conscience. I only see Max. His handsome face, his beautiful soul. He's perfect. He's everything I didn't know I wanted, and finally, he's made the move that proves he wants me in return. He isn't afraid of me. And with him, I don't feel like

I need to be afraid of myself. My chest could burst with happiness.

When I find him at the piano, he takes my waist in one hand and the back of my head in the other and pulls me into a passionate kiss.

When our faces finally separate, he moves his lips to my ear. "Let's get out of here," he breathes in a timid whisper.

Lillian, Max, and I exit the speakeasy into the crisp New York night, where they explain to me that Max's flight from Boston to London had been canceled because of the snow. Almost all the flights were full, but he was able to book a red-eye, going out of New York's LaGuardia Airport a week from now. In the meantime, he decided he would visit his brother in Manhattan. When he texted Lillian to see where her place was in proximity to Ollie's, she asked him if he wanted to meet up. He'd been thinking the same thing but wasn't sure how I would feel about it. They devised a plan that involved an old family friend's piano bar, and the rest was simple—keep the secret for twelve hours, which actually wasn't so simple for Lillian. But miraculously, she held her tongue.

"So now what?" I ask enthusiastically, thrilled to be in such an exciting city, with my two favorite people.

"Well, I'm actually catching up with some people from high school soon… I wanted to give you two some alone time." She smirks, hailing a cab.

It pulls up, and she opens the door for us, and ushers us inside before we can protest. Then she says "83rd and Park Ave" to the driver, shuts the door and shoos us away with a wave goodbye.

Back at Lillian's place, nerves nip at the lining of my stomach, despite the wine Max and I consumed when we returned. The only time I've ever shown Max my body was to admonish myself, to scare him away. Now, I'm supposed to be enticing him. I've never done this with someone who I actually care about what they might think of my appearance. I feel safe, but I don't feel beautiful.

I slowly peel the clothes from my body and discard them in a pile on the guest bedroom floor, like a writhing snake, shedding its skin. I shiver.

"Cold?" Max asks, pulling off his shirt. I nod. "Come here," he says with inviting warmth. I step towards where he sits on the edge of the bed. He gently places his hands over my shoulders and rubs them softly to warm me, but not to hurt me. He looks at me like he's appreciating a work in a museum. He moves his hands down my arms to hold my hands.

"You're so beautiful," he whispers, reaching up and brushing the hair from my eyes.

His face is glazed with affection. I remember what he told me, about considering perspective. I need to believe he finds me attractive. I let my breath go.

It feels good to relax. Only now am I able to fully admire his body on display before me. His features are fine like art. His body is chiseled and smooth. Something stirs in me, heavy like wet paint. I move my face to Max's and push my tongue into his mouth, molding my lips to his. His hands canvas my breasts and waist. Then he moves to squeeze my butt and picks me up from under my legs. He turns around and lays me down on the sheet. He traces a line down my abdomen with a trail of kisses. Then he dips his tongue into me, spinning. Warmth bleeds through my body like ink. A moan drips from my lips. I take his head in my hands and draw him to my face. He lets out a sigh as he carefully carves himself like stone into the stretch of my legs. He smoothly paints himself in and out of my body with thick, broad strokes while he squeezes me in his arms. I feel a colorful palette of emotion spray through my mind: the orange hues of happiness, the red shades of pleasure. I hang onto the edge of the mattress as they pulse through me.

Afterwards I admire Max next to me in the bed, right where I'd imagined him the night before.

"I can't believe you're here," I think out loud.

"I know. I can't believe my stupid serenade worked." He laughs.

"It was so romantic – it was like something out of a movie. How could it not be?" I point out.

"I don't know, I was starting to get worried we would never be more than just friends," he admits.

"At heart, we were never just friends." I grin.

"This is true. I was actually going to give you this in the coffee shop, but I wasn't sure how you'd take it," he says, reaching down into the pocket of his pants, which sit on the floor. Then he takes my hand and places a small gold locket in my hands.

I look at him with appreciation. "Max, where did you get this?" I ask, trying to avoid asking *how*.

"I picked it up last week," he says proudly.

"It's too nice," I shake my head. "I can't accept it."

"It's okay; it would make me happy if you would."

"How did you…" I ask, needing to know.

"I saved some tips and borrowed the rest from Ollie," he says casually. "I'll be squared off soon enough, don't worry about it."

I look into his eyes with guilty gratitude. "Thank you." I tell him, but I want to tell him more. A sugary feeling tingles in my chest and spins up into my face. I want to tell him I've never felt so overwhelmingly happy around anyone before. That he gives me enough hope to undo a lifetime of fear. That every ounce of real pain I now feel is worth the warmth he brings to my life. I want to tell him I love him.

I flip my hair to the side and move to bring the clasp of the locket around my neck.

"Here–" he smiles, and clasps it clumsily around my neck, then sits back and touches the locket as if he's making sure it's real. He looks at me satisfied. Suddenly, his face grows serious, but not upset. He only looks like he needs to give me very important instructions.

"Julia," he says softly as I give him my undivided attention, "I know this feels fast, but I feel like I've known you for years. You're not like these other people all around us– you're not obsessed with money or status or image. You're not some facade of a human. You're authentic. You make me feel more sure of myself than anyone. And I want you to know that," he takes a deep breath, "I really, truly love you."

My heart swells. *One step ahead of me.*

"I love you too."

14.

The week goes on, and I find myself growing tired of the taste of my own name on my tongue as I introduce myself to fistfuls of people I will likely never meet a second time. It doesn't help that Max is wildly friendly and talks to everyone: waiters at restaurants, strangers on the subway, Lillian's high school friends—everyone. And they all ask me one thing: what do you do? Max and I agree that this is a foolish question. What people should be asking is, *what are you passionate about?* The problem is, I'm still figuring out my own answer to that question, so I'll just keep telling people my name in the meantime.

"Hi, I'm Julia," I say nervously to someone
I actually do hope to meet again someday.

"Hi, Julia, I'm Oliver, and this is my
partner, Chance. It's so lovely to meet you!" Oliver
says, taking off his long wool coat and hanging it on
his dining chair. He looks just like Max, but slightly
shorter with a bit more polish around the edges. His
hair is freshly trimmed and styled. His shirt is
pressed. His watch and wedding band have been
recently shined. His teeth are bleached, and he smells
of aftershave and cologne. His posture is tight.

"It's nice to meet you both." I smile, as
Oliver takes my right hand in both of his own and
gives me a firm welcoming handshake, before
moving to hug Max around the end of the table. I
turn to Chance and smile awkwardly.

"Oh, get in here." He motions for me to
give him a hug. He smells expensive in a unisexy way.
I stand up and give him a limp, crooked squeeze,
there in the crammed, cozy restaurant.

"Look how pretty you are!" Chance says, stepping back and admiring me, "Max, why didn't you tell us just how pretty she is!" I redden.

"Stop that, Chance; you'll scare her off," Oliver scolds. We all sit down at the table.

"Fine, we'll stick to things Max *did* tell us," I freeze, considering what those things could be. "We heard you're studying poetry; how's that going?"

"Good," I exhale, "I'm graduating this spring, actually."

"Really, what are your plans afterwards?" Chance presses.

"I'm not really sure," I tell him.

"Well, if you ever consider song writing, just give me a call! Here," he perks up, and shuffles around in his coat pocket, which he hasn't been focused enough to remove yet, "take this!" He hands me his card. His kindness makes my nervous chills dissipate.

"Thank you." I smile, take it from his well-manicured hand, and stow it away safely in my purse.

"No problem, and you know, you can write from anywhere, Boston, New York, even… London." He looks back and forth between Max and me, his shaped eyebrows raised in promiscuous excitement.

Max breathes out a little laugh.

The thought of moving to London suddenly makes me gregarious. I give Max a sparkling glance.

"If you choose London, then I'll be all alone in New York!" Max gently prods me with his forearm.

"Hang on, are you planning on moving to the city after your MBA?" Oliver asks, delight riding on his surprise.

"I mean that would be the goal. This is the best place to find a job in most types of business," Max points out.

"Yeah, and the worst," Chance chimes in, "I have friends who wear diapers under their suits so they don't have to waste time using the bathroom during their fourteen-hour workdays."

Max looks impartial—dismissive and smiling, like he doesn't want to linger on this topic for too long.

"I've got a bladder of iron," he jokes.

"And a heart of gold. You're not built for the trenches of Wall Street," Chance frames Max's face between his thumbs like he's aiming an imaginary camera at him, "now, behind the keys of a piano, that's where I see you."

Max smiles at him politely, but I watch as a small mournful flare flashes across his face.

After dinner, as I'm coming back from the bathroom, I see Max from across the restaurant. His eyes have darkened since I left. I slow my pace and watch him and Oliver, now alone, from between the cover of the other tables, wondering what he's talking about. The only clues I can have are in his hands. He moves one over his eyes momentarily before throwing it in the air, angrily making a point about something. I find myself stopping next to an obnoxious tropical-looking plant, sitting before the final stretch of the restaurant leading back to our table. Max's expression slowly sours from a dark intensity to a look of gloomy sadness—as if he may cry.

"It's a shame, isn't it?" A voice jolts behind me, rattling my concentration. I turn to look at Chance, standing behind me, struck with pity. I look at him receptively, concealing the truth of my unawareness of what he means by this. He continues.

"I mean, what had it been? Ten years since Claire got sober? And just like that, a decade of hard work, gone with one moment of weakness,"

My heart sinks. Claire must be Max's mom.

"And now they had to go and change their flights from Heathrow to Manchester at the last minute. What a nightmare."

I nod, better understanding the events of the week.

"And now Theodore is being difficult, saying he wants the boys for Christmas." Chance shakes his head. "You'll understand when you meet him. Sometimes he's all head and no heart," he says.

Suddenly, Max looks up at us. Like a professional, he slaps on a shiny new grin and waves us over. We start toward them.

"You know," Chance whispers to me out of the corner of his mouth, "Max is lucky to have you. You've been making him really happy."

This touches my heart. I smile a grateful smile in his direction before sitting back next to Max.

When we've said goodbye to Oliver and Chance, Max asks, "What do you think? I could use another drink, but we could always grab a cab if you're tired," Max asks me.

"Actually, I think we should grab one more drink. There's a place just down the street I'm really wanting to check out," I suggest.

"I'm down for that," he says, wrapping his arm around my shoulders. "What's it called?" he asks.

"You'll see," I grin.

"Oh my!" Max laughs when we arrive outside the pub. "The Dead Poet." He reads out loud, amused.

We grab a small table in the back of the pub.

"How did you discover this place?" Max asks.

"When I was getting directions over here, I spotted it on my map," I explain to him with a hint of pride.

"Well, I'm glad you did. This place is great," he praises, taking a sip of his beer and looking around at the comical juxtaposition of old novels piled in nooks next to framed quotes, mainly in reference to alcohol inspired humor, that hang along the walls.

"Why do you like it so much?" I ask.

"The beer?" he responds.

"The book," I clarify, "we never talked about why it was one of your favorites."

"Ah," he nods, and then stays silent for a few moments, choosing his words. "I guess not only do I appreciate the message about seizing the day, but I can relate to the characters. I feel some pressure to not only make my parents proud, but also to prove that I'm stronger than what happened in my life."

"Is that why you're going to business school? Do you think it will help you prove that to yourself?" I press.

He scoffs at himself, "I think that going to business school will prove that to my dad." The color seems to drain from his cheeks. He drops his head. His honesty is heavy in my heart.

"But what are you trying to prove to yourself?" I ask.

He looks at me with a self-sacrificial nobility.

"What I want doesn't matter," he says.

I've never seen him like this before—vulnerable. It's always been him giving me advice, not the other way around. But he looks at me now with a familiar desperation. I know how it feels to look for hope in the eyes of another person. Empathy compels me to locate some vault of wisdom in my bank of limited emotional intelligence.

"Exactly." I agree.

"What?" he asks.

"You're exactly right. You're proving to yourself in going to business school for your dad that what you want doesn't matter. That your father's approval is where your value lies, and that your self-worth is based on that."

He looks down at the table for a long moment, then back up at me.

"Julia, you're right," he says, realization fresh in his tone. "This whole time, I thought I was proving to my dad that I was better than him—better than the job he couldn't get, better than the divorce papers, and the late bills, the court hearings. Better than the MBA he talked about, but never pursued. But all along, I was proving to myself that what I was on my own, separate from my father's expectations, wasn't enough. I thought I had to outdo someone else for me to feel fulfilled, and I was so focused on that I haven't stopped to think about what it is I actually want for me," he looks at me electrified, "I'm quitting business school. I'm going to be a composer."

There he is. I want to let out a great *barbaric yawp* of support, like the boys do in *Dead Poets Society*, but a twinge of apprehension suffocates me. The last thing I want to do is drive a nail between Max and his father. I give him an encouraging nod but I clench the burden of truth between my teeth. He reads my hesitation, written on my face like a warning.

"My dad isn't going to be happy," he admits.

I open my jaw like a cage and set the words free. He needs to hear this.

"Following your heart can be painful, but living for someone else will eventually hurt more. You have to live for yourself, or you'll never truly be happy."

As the words leave my lips and something eats at me. My appetite for introspection has awakened– I can't help but wonder if this advice better serves Max, or myself.

Max interrupts my unsettling thought.

"Julia, can I ask you something?"

I smile, pulling myself from this hungry anxiety that stalks me from the back of my mind. "Anything."

"We don't have to talk about this if you don't want to, but while we're talking about dads, I was wondering… and tell me if I'm out of line, but I was wondering… what happened to your father?"

The question pounces on me. I knew it would come someday. And in encouraging Max to face his own familial qualms, I set it up for him like bait. He opened up, and now it's my turn.

"Okay," I say, "I'll tell you, but I'm going to need another beer."

I start from the beginning, with William Wright's family history of mental illness—his father's abusive tendencies, his mother's overdose at the age of forty-five, which was likely suicidal. How he adored his mother, Julia, and how he would go on to name his own daughter after her. How she left everything to him in her will. I tell him how William married Jaqueline Hearst, practically as a favor to his boss, before he knew the company was going bankrupt, and never really loved his wife, per her own accord. I tell him how William adored his daughter, how he taught her to read when she was only four years old, and how proud he was of this. How they would spend nights together by the fire as he braided her hair and she read him stories. By the time she was eight, she was reading chapter books. Then I tell him how one night, in the dead of winter, deep into a bottle of whisky, he snapped. I tell him, with tears in my eyes, how he beat his precious daughter half to death, how she was in the hospital for three weeks, and how when she got out, he was gone. How she would later learn from a drunken Jaqueline that William Wright had shot himself in the head. How he'd left a note with his will to her, admitting that he couldn't live with himself after hurting his daughter the way he had. I tell him how this would have lasting effects on the daughter. How for every couple of years she seemed to be okay, she would spend a week in a psychiatric facility, not because she'd begun hurting herself again, but because she'd been caught. I tell him how doctors theorize that the girl's last ties to her suddenly departed father was rooted in abuse and that in her shock, her brain decided that in some twisted way, the pain associated with abusing herself brings her the comfort of his memory. The comfort of love. That, to the girl, love was pain. Until she met a boy who showed her that love can be separate from pain, and that if she can get through the pains of life, she can appreciate the beauty in love.

When I'm done with my story, I notice that Max, too, has streams of tears rolling down his cheeks.

The next afternoon, I say my goodbyes to Max, Oliver and Chance, as they depart for their flight to London.

When I get back to Lillian's apartment, she's waiting on the couch for me, concealing something long and skinny, like a pen, in the clutches of both her hands.

"Hey, is that my Christmas present?" I joke, going over to her.

"No," she sniffles, and I now see that her pale face is streaked with inky, mascara-tinted tears. "I think it's mine."

She parts her fingers to reveal a plastic white stick with a blue cap on one end and an plus sign on the other.

"I'm pregnant."

15.

It's a cold, forlorn ride back to Boston. After Christmas, I give Lillian a few days to tell her parents the news—that she is pregnant, most likely, with Jerrod Kaminski's child. That she wants to keep the baby, despite what she thinks they will probably tell her she should do. That she's going to have to drop out of the MBA program she never really wanted to do in the first place.

I stare at my thumbs, reflecting back on what a menace I've been lately in the inspiration department. In the last week, I've advised both Max and Lillian to follow their hearts and stay true to themselves at the expense of their responsibilities. The irony is that if I were told by someone to stay true to myself, I would not even know how I might do that, nor do I have any responsibility to betray. I don't need to be getting an MFA for some prospective career goal. I have no obligation to my mother. I don't have to worry about money, status, or appearance. I don't even need to hurt myself anymore to cope with the insignificant stresses of life. The only thing I seem to need now is Max. And I'm beginning to worry that he only wants me for the things I am not. And when you take away what I am not, there's not a whole lot left.

Who am I, I wonder.

———————————

When I make it back to my apartment and go to reclaim Fish from my neighbors, there's a sad surprise that awaits me.

"Julia," the woman says, holding a dry, empty bowl, "I'm so sorry, but while you were away, Fish… he's dead."

My heart sinks as any anticipation of returning to a positive normalcy in Lillian and Max's absence wiggles away from me in front of my eyes. Back in my apartment, tears bubble to my surface.

For the last week that Max has been gone, he's called me every day. He still hasn't mentioned his mom's relapse, so I don't press him. I just try to comfort him. Yesterday, he told me that tomorrow he would be breaking the news to his dad that he no longer wants to get his Master's degree in Business. This is now today. I anxiously keep my eye on the phone throughout the day, late into the night, but he never calls. Same thing the next day. I know he's flying back, so I think that maybe he's become preoccupied with his travels. On the third day, a petrifying fear punches me in the gut as my phone finally rings, with Max's name spread across the screen. Something sour starts to swim in me.

"Hello?" I answer.

"Julia," his voice is sweet in my ear after not hearing it for days, "I'm on my way over to you… We need to talk." He speaks, fragile, as if he may shatter me if he talks too harshly. I lower the phone from the side of my face and hang up.

His words hang above my head like a guillotine. *We need to talk.* What else could that mean?

I'm suddenly overcome with a chaotic urge to clean. I begin frantically shoving my laundry in drawers, aligning the items on my dresser and making my bed. Then, I run to my bathroom and vomit briskly in the toilet, tidy that up, then sweep a few items from my counter into my vanity. I pace across my apartment in a dizzy panic, to the living room. I straighten out and fluff the pillows on my couch on my way to the kitchen, where I pump soap into my hand and start scrubbing a dirty plate with great intensity. I rinse the suds from its surface and my hands, then fill my palms with water and splash my face. As I'm drying off, there's a knock on the door. I swing it open impatiently.

Max stands, wilting in the doorway, his dark eyes focused on his feet. I step to the side and allow him to enter my apartment, and slowly, he walks over and sits down at my kitchen table. I join him and scan his poker face for answers. I know what is happening. Now, the only question I have is *why*. I don't know how to ask this, so I wait for him to speak. He takes his time. Eventually, a clumsy line tumbles from his lips like falling dominos.

"Julia, I don't know how to say this, but I can't– we can't be together anymore. I'm sorry, I need to focus on school and if I don't, I could lose my scholarship and, I'm sorry we just can't."

I have only one response to this betrayal, and that is silence. Shock sits on my words and traps them in my body. What I can't say begins foaming in me. It clings to my insides, bubbling and churning in my stomach. Steamy panic rises up from my core, stews my chest, and licks my neck and face. I'm afraid I'm going to vomit again.

I stand up from the table and walk to the kitchen sink, where I bend over and rest my head on my folded arms on the edge of the counter. I close my eyes and try to find my breath but it feels as if someone has sucked all the air from the room. I feel Max's hand on my back and I flinch, but stay with my head down in my arms.

"I'm sorry, Julia, it's not personal, it's just–"

"It's not personal?" I whirl up as a strong blow of anger whistles in my ears. "What do you mean it's not personal?" I burst out in disbelief.

"It's just I—"

"Was it personal when we sat on the floor of that study, talking about pain and death and hope? Was it personal when we kissed? Was it personal when you played my poetry to your piano? Was it personal when you told me I was beautiful? That I was unlike anyone you'd ever met? " I move my own face close to his own. "Was it personal when you told me you loved me? Because I don't know about *you*, but that was personal to *me*."

Tears glaze Max's eyes as he stares at me with pitiful silence. I can't stand to look at him. I throw my hands up over my eyes and back away.

"God, how could I have been so stupid?!" I yell into the air.

"You weren't stupid," Max whispers.

I wind back to him. "You know what? You're right," I jab a finger in his direction, "I wasn't stupid for believing you. You were so convincing with your bullshit. 'Try everything,'" I mock him.

"Julia, I'm sorry I just can't fix this!" he yells. Then he looks down and whispers "I can't fix you."

My ears burn. I look at him with deep disgust. "'Fix' me?" I ask, appalled. "I didn't ask you to fix me!" I yell. Then, with a little gasp, it hits me. "I get it now," I claim. "'Try everything'," I repeat. "Well, you tried to fix me, and you realized you couldn't. Just like you couldn't fix your mom," I singe into his ego with a burning hot brand of theories. "And now that you've had your fun playing a struggling, love-struck musician abroad, it's time to throw your fantasy and everything in it away and go back to being a good little businessman like your dad wants you to be." All of these words don't sound like my own and taste vile leaving my mouth, like poison.

Hurting, Max looks at me, his dark eyes like the tips of two pistol barrels. "Well, I'm sorry I have to actually worry about my financial future because my dad didn't kill himself to leave me all of his money!" he shoots.

I target a deep glare at him as his words ring in my ears. Tears fall from my narrowed eyes like bullet casings. A horrible pressure begins to build in me. It's a distantly familiar itch, one that hasn't plagued me like this in weeks, but still sickens me at its slightest resurgence. This craving for a painful antidote sends me flying into a panic and the urge to ground myself multiplies and swarms inside me like wasps smoked from a nest.

"I would give all the money in the world to have my dad back," I fire. I blaze past him, heading from the kitchen to the living room, attempting to flee this buzzing hunger building in me.

He calls after me, "Julia, wait, I didn't mean that; it just slipped out. I'm sorry, I–"

"Don't worry," I say, spinning back around, "I won't take anything you say seriously now that I know it's all lies anyway."

"But it wasn't all lies," he cries. I see that his knuckles are bruised and cut, like he's been fighting for his life. But his face is clean. He's been fighting with himself. "I still love you."

His words pierce me. I shake my head in confusion and step towards him. "Then why are you leaving me?" I ask.

He stares at me for a moment, then steps forward, embracing me in his arms. I know that it's a hug goodbye. Grief roils in me. I can't contain my urges any longer. *I can't.*

"Hit me," I whisper, shaking.

"What?" Max asks.

"Hit me," I say, louder this time.

"*Hit* you?" Max clarifies, concern in his voice.

I push his arms from me, bursting out of the hug. "Hit me!" I shout.

"No!" Max retaliates, backing away, confused.

"Hit me! Hit me!" The screams erupt from my mouth, as I inch towards him, desperate to feel something other than the pain of him leaving. He just watches me, his face melted with sorrow.

"Please just hit me, hit me!" I beg between sobs.

Suddenly, his brows furrow and he changes his course, stepping forward. He looks at me with pursed lips. He lowers his chin and then raises his arm above his shoulder, as if he's winding up for a slap. My heart jumps with the anticipation of relief. I take a quick breath in and as I exhale, I open my chest, relax my shoulders and close my eyes and wait. But the sting of the slap never comes. Only the feeling of Max's big hand holding my face, tenderly. He swipes tears from my cheek with his thumb. I feel his lips press against my forehead. *One step ahead of me.* Then I hear footsteps, and my front door opening and closing.

He's gone.

I feel very stiff, like I'm made of wood. I sit down on the floor next to my couch and stay very still for a very long time, trying to remember words and what they mean. But I can only remember a few, and those I do manage to remember mean nothing. *Love* means nothing. *Pain* means nothing. *Hope* means nothing. There are no answers because I can not even find the words to ask a question. I have no solid thoughts. Only dribbling, liquid concepts rush through my head. They fall from my eyes and slide down my neck. When I try to hold them, they slip between my fingers and evaporate, back into the thick cloud that is my brain. They float around, unsubsidized, lost.

16.

At some point, I must have crawled to my bed because I wake up there the next morning. I drag myself to the bathroom and pee—a hollow victory, but a victory nonetheless. I go back to my bed and lie down, but I'm too sad to sleep and too tired to cry. I just lie there, existing, in some half-conscious purgatory between reality and the incomprehension of.

When I muster enough courage to reflect on what has just happened between Max and me, this awareness makes me ill. I want to crawl out of my body.

How could Max have told me all those things, made me feel so happy, and taken it all away in an instant? Max's dad must've talked some serious sense into him when he brought up the idea of dropping out of business school. *I pushed him too far*, I think. His mom's relapse must've shaken his faith in hope. He saw the truth. That no matter how hard you try, you cannot hope away the pain. Why couldn't I have just sat with my pain? Why did I have to go and replace it with something far more dangerous— love? I can't sit with this feeling. *I can't.*

I stand up and walk to my kitchen, pour myself a glass of whiskey, and gulp it down with burning desire. I pushed myself too far as well, into places I would've never gone on my own. I stretched my luck, and it snapped. And now I'm stuck here, in this place where I have no comfort in pain and find no beauty in love. My whole life, I've been seeking out pain in every minute of every day. In every crack and crevice. In every flavor, temperature, and tone. And now that I'm free from this craving, here it is. Right in front of me. The greatest pain I've ever felt

—heartbreak. *Gulp*. I can't even take pleasure in that. I have nothing. If only I hadn't been so inspired. Then I would've never fallen for any of this. *Gulp*. I refill my glass and bring it with me over to my desk, where I dig up a notecard and single out a pen. Then I scribble out a message.

> *When the day is done and the sun has set*
> *And I'm taking in my final breath*
> *Just promise me this: you will carry on*
> *And know that you were my swan song*

I pull out an envelope and stuff the letter inside. Then I wrench the gold locket from my neck and drop that inside too, and address the package to Max. I run downstairs and plop it in my building outbound mail chute. In the mail room is a package addressed to me. I snatch it up and tear it open on my way back up the stairs. Inside are two rolled-up red wads of boxing wraps. It's the Christmas gift I'd ordered Max, just now arriving.

I hear a laugh skip from my lips back in my apartment as I empty the package, letting the wraps tumble to the floor in the center of my room. Then, as I discard the thick folder to the side, I spy *Dead Poets Society* sitting at the top of a pile of books on my desk. I walk over to it and pick it up. I look at it with grief, that spins into anger. I hurl it across the room. It hits Fish's empty bowl on my dresser, knocking it to the ground, shattering it and spilling blue gravel and broken glass across the floor. *That felt good.*

I reach back to my desk and grab the next book in the pile. *The Bell Jar.* My face squeezes itself into a twisted scowl as I glimpse the disgusting brown part where I'd cut my fingers across the paper, and tear the pages frantically in handfuls from the spine of the book. I discard them on the floor around my feet, like leaves falling from a tree.

Then I turn to *The Complete Poems of Emily Dickinson*, pick it up, and chuck it at my bookshelf with all of my might. From the corner of my eye, I watch as something shiny slips from the shelf and lands with a *clank* on the wood floor.

I walk over to the foot of the furniture, whiskey in hand, and pick up the bronze letter cutter from the ground. I kick back my chin with my glass to my mouth and down the rest of my drink, then toss the vessel to the side with a *thud*.

Then, I bring the feather with me into my bathroom and set it on the edge of the tub before cranking on the water, which gurgles from the faucet in a thick, powerful vein. I'm compelled to get in before the basin is full. I undress. As I step over the porcelain wall, warmth gathers around my ankles, and dresses me in a moment of calm as I lower myself into the bath. A yearning to preserve this feeling washes across my consciousness. I only consider one way to do this.

I spread apart my legs and scoot myself closer to the faucet so that the warm water rushes between my thighs. A steady itch for more throbs through my insides. I bring my legs up onto the wall and angle myself downward so that the pressure of the flow is even more direct. I grip the sides of the tub and throw my head back in satisfaction. My legs quiver and shake and I realize I'm moaning. I float my hips up and down as I fulfill these all-encompassing urges. "Oh, god," I hear myself say as I teeter on the edge of climax. "Oh, god, please" I beg. "Oh god!" I squeal in quick breaths as I reach the peak of pleasure.

Then, slowly, my smile melts into a frown as reality begins to creep back into my mind. "Oh god," I say again, though my self-enjoyment has expired. I wrench off the water and roll to my side in the half-full bath. The breath in my lungs ceases to slow and tears begin to leak from my eyes. "Oh god," I cry out, "Please, god, please!" I sob so uncontrollably that I must grab onto the side of the tub for stability. My hand touches something cold—the feather. It breaks me from my trance.

Slowly, I recover from my composure enough to stare into notched veins of the tool's detailing. My heart pounds in my ears. I think about the love I used to feel for pain. How I've become such a dirty hypocrite. How Sylvia Plath would hate me for this and how I'll never escape my own bell jar.

I think about my mom and how she's certainly not thinking about me back. I think about Max's dad and what he might've said to make Max take back everything he gave me. I think about his stupid, cheesy swan song. I think about how stupid I was for believing him and for believing myself when I'd hoped I could be happy with the love he'd shown me. I think about how selfish I was to try and persuade him to do what I thought was right when I had no business telling him what to do with this. How he didn't bother taking my advice anyway. How after all this, I'm right back where I started but without the only thing that kept me going before. The reliable, grounding, beautiful enjoyment of pain. I move the letter opener to my wrist. Then I curl in my lips and close my eyes tight and slice. I copy the motion, pasting a mirrored cut on the other wrist, and drop the cutter to the side.

At first, I feel nothing. The adrenaline masks any present pain. Then slowly a sore untroublesome throbbing begins to pulse to the beat of my heart. I watch, mesmerized as blood salivates from the open mouths of the gashes. It drools down my wrists and seeps into the water, turning it red.

I sit there, bathing, in my own tears, blood and pity. A slight grin turns my lips. The end of my suffering is in sight. Now, *this* is beautiful. My head grows light. I close my eyes and breathe a sigh of relief as I approach my peace. I think about Max and how he'll go on to finish business school. And Lillian and how she won't. How she'll be such an amazing mother to her baby that I'll never meet. How she took such good care of me and how I was nothing but selfish to her. How I'm just like my mother–always thinking about myself. I think about all the things I would've done differently. How I would've been a better friend. A better partner. A better daughter. I think about my dad, and how this is how he must've felt before he pulled the trigger. How he'd been so regretful of hurting me, that he could not bear to live.

Suddenly, a panic pulls me back from my reflection. My father—he died for what he'd done to hurt me. And all I've done in return, every day since then, is hurt myself. I *am* selfish. Not only to others, but I'm selfish towards myself. And I proved to myself, in these last months, that I have the power to overcome this. Max wasn't my cure. It wasn't him that made me stop hurting myself. It was *me*. With his encouragement, of course, I decided *I* would find hope in life. That *I* would beat my addiction to pain. My whole life, I've burdened others and myself with the very thing my father killed himself over—my pain. He killed himself because he wanted me to escape it. I can't kill myself. *I can't.* His sacrifice would be in vain. My potential would be squandered. The only way to lose hope for certain is to give up for good. *I hope.*

My eyes shoot open. The room is blurry and spinning. I move to hold my wrists closed, but it's useless. I feel warm blood as it spills through my cold, tingly fingers. I need to get out of this tub. I try to flail my arms and legs awake, but I'm losing consciousness. I gasp for any morsel of oxygen but the weight of death sits on my neck, smothering me, gagging me with it's heavy, cold, hands. Suddenly, a brightness blinds me, and a deafening silence sits flat in my ears. A shadow, one of a man, appears above me.

"Dad?" I ask, horrified and moved all at once. "Daddy, I'm so sorry."

17.

When I open my eyes, everything is white and fuzzy. A glowing golden angel stares at me.

"Julia?" it asks in a quiet voice, "Oh my God, Julia!" it cries and hugs me tight.

I blink myself awake. I smell a familiar sweet perfume that brings me to full consciousness.

"Lillian?"

She hugs me, sobbing. "I'm so sorry Julia, I didn't know that asshole would break your heart, I should've been there, I'm so sorry–"

"Lillian, where are we?" I ask, trying to piece together previous happenings.

"We're in the intensive care unit. Your mom was here earlier, but she ran out for lunch. You were almost dead when they found you," she recounts, skipping between answers to questions I didn't ask.

"They?"

"The cops—I guess the neighbors called 911 when they heard crashing and screaming. They got there just in time." She pauses and redirects a trickle of tears that runs down her face with her hand. "There's another thing," she tells me, sniffing and looking down and pulling out her phone. "They said that these saved your life." She holds the screen up, reflecting an image of two bloodied dark red strips of fabric laid out on a sterile table next to a measuring stick. It's the boxing wraps. I look down at my wrists, cuffed in thick white bandages, as a deep shame erupts in my face. A long silence wafts in the air.

Eventually, Lillian speaks.

"Why do the people we love the most end up being the ones that hurt us?" She asks, shaking her head in disbelief. I think about this for a long moment, then I look at her.

"I think it hurts so much *because* we love them the most." A sad smile rises on the horizon of my lips. "But there's something beautiful about that. About caring about someone so much that it hurts. That it hurts to stay, but you do it anyway. That it hurts to leave because you love what you're leaving, but it hurts more to sit in one place than to go. That no matter how much you might hurt during this change, you will learn. Learn to conquer this pain. Learn to overcome the fear. You will learn to hope."

My cheeks burn. But something else starts to bloom between the cracks of my deep abashment. A flowering gratitude. A beautiful, distant but powerful, untouchable hope.

When I'm discharged, my mom takes me back to my apartment and I catalog the mess I've made.

"I would've sent someone to clean up honey, but I didn't have a key," she tells me, coming back from parking the car. I don't bother telling her the door was unlocked. I have a lot of work to do.

I walk into the bathroom and kneel at the foot of the tub. Then I dip my hand into the blood bath and fish out the opener, and once again, wash it.

"I'm going to grab some groceries," I tell my mom, who's sprawled out on the couch.

"Oh, pick me up a bottle of wine would you, honey?"

"Okay," I nod.

Then, I put on my coat, take out the trash and walk to Jerrod's brownstone, where I approach the front door. This time, there are no fake bouncers. I drop the letter opener in the mailbox.

As I'm leaving, I catch a glimpse of something moving in the window. At first, I think it might be Mr. and Mrs. Kaminski. But then, through the warm lights of the foyer, I see the pink-dipped ends of Lillian's golden hair as she slowly sways back and forth with Jerrod in delicate dance.

I smile a fragile smile, as the tip of my nose starts to sting in the winter night.

EPILOGUE

I try not to throw up from nerves on the subway ride to the Upper West Side. David Bowie's *Golden Years* blasts in my earphones for courage as I ruffle my short brown hair with my fingers in the reflection of the subway car window before the train screeches to a halt and the doors disappear into the narrow cavity of the train's frame.

"This is 86th and Broadway," a staticky voice booms from the loudspeaker as I hop out of the car and onto the platform. "Next stop is 96th Street; stand clear of the closing doors."

I'm finally starting to become fluent in the language of subway conductor, I realize. I put my hand in my pocket and crinkle the envelope for the one-hundredth time. *Still there*, I confirm as I climb the stairs out of the subway and into the autumn New York night. I look around me, studying the shop-lined streets of Broadway. Even after almost two years here, I've barely scratched the surface of my exploratory potential.

Tonight, I won't be making any progress down my citywide bucket list, as I'm revisiting an old place. But tonight is not just about the future; it's also about the past. My stomach turns as I come upon my destination. I take a deep breath as I enter the doors of The Dead Poet Pub.

She's already there, in the back, sitting at our table. She looks even more beautiful than the night I thought I'd lost her. Her light brown hair has grown out long, past her shoulders. She's gained a few pounds so that she looks healthier than ever. Her eyes, the colour of emeralds, stand out against her black clothing. Her cheeks glow in the warmth of the bar.

"Julia," I say with amazement reaching my arms out as I approach her.

"Max," she replies, standing up and accepting my embrace before stepping back. "Look at you, you look good." She gestures to my entirety with her gaze.

We sit down.

"How have you been?" she asks. Her voice is hypnotic.

"I've been good; I was glad when you called," I tell her with honesty.

"I was surprised you hadn't," she replies with a bit of wit and a lot of charm.

"I wasn't sure you'd want to see me; I was an asshole," I admit.

"You were, but I assume it was complicated," she says, looking down.

"It was." I agree. I think back to my dad's warnings… and threats. I look down at my own calloused fingers. "But in the end, you were right," I tell her.

"I was?" she asks with a sparkle in those bright green eyes.

"You were. I finished business school… Like my dad told me," I laugh a little at my foolishness, "but when I graduated, and was looking for jobs, I couldn't stop thinking about what you told me– how I couldn't live for someone else, and if I tried to, I would never be truly happy."

She smiles a beaming grin at me. "So what are you doing in the city now?" she asks.

"I'm actually a bartender," I smile, "But only by night. By day, I'm teaching piano and composing my own music." I smirk.

She looks at me with proud happiness.

"And how's your mom?" she asks quietly, as if she doesn't want to know if the answer is not *good*.

"She's really good." I nod. "What about Lillian? I think I saw on my old roommate's socials that she just got married?"

"Yes! To Jerrod!" she says happily.

"That's brilliant." My heart warms.

"Yeah, everyone knew they would end up together before they did. Turns out, they just needed a baby to bring them together. One might call it a little, or maybe really big, push to commitment." She giggles.

"Somehow that makes perfect sense," I laugh. "What about you? Are you in town for the wedding?"

"Partially. But I'm staying another week because I'm also here for an interview with a label. I'm hoping to be brought on as a freelance songwriter," she tells me. Passion flickers across her face.

"Really?" I ask.

"Yeah, actually, Chance is the one that reached out to me to let me know a position was opening up," she tells me.

"Did he?" I ask, surprised. I'd just seen Chance and Ollie the other night for dinner, and Chance hadn't mentioned anything. *That cheeky bugger*, I think.

"Yeah, when he mentioned you were in town, I knew I needed to reach out, because I never said thank you."

"Thank you? For what, breaking your heart?" I ask, my confusion growing by the second.

"For saving my life," she corrects me. *She knows*, I think, shocked.

"How did you…" my voice trails off as I consider all the ways she might have learned that I was there that night.

"EMTs don't use boxing wraps to stop bleeding, they carry bandages for that, and my neighbors have never called the cops before, no matter how much noise I've made."

I take a deep breath.

"After I'd had a few days away from my dad, I realized the weight he'd had on my decision. Just as he'd always done, he convinced me to do something I didn't really want to do."

"So you came back?" she asks, her words drenched in emotion.

"I did. Just in time, too," I say, trying to keep my voice from shaking. "You had stopped breathing when I got there. I pulled you from the tub." I can't hold in the tears. "I called 911 and used the wraps to slow the bleeding, but it wasn't enough. I gave you CPR until the EMTs arrived."

Julia wipes a tear from her cheek. "I'm sorry you had to see that," she musters.

"No, *I'm* sorry." I apologize with as much sympathy as I can manage to communicate.

I'm overwhelmed with an urge to hold her in my arms and keep her safe from the world, just like before. But I have the feeling she no longer needs holding. Still, I want to. But I know a million *I'm sorry*s will never be enough to make up for the way I left her.

"I have something to tell you too," I say, swallowing my pride, "I've thought about you every day since then… and I have regrets."

"I don't," she says, matter-of-factly.

My heart sinks.

She continues, "I don't have regrets because I finally saw what I needed to see in order to want to live a life of hope for myself, instead of relying on everyone around me. The way you left may have hurt me, but I also have to acknowledge that it helped me. And so did everything else you did for me beforehand. I can't forget about that part of what we had. You're the one that told me; you can't judge a person based only on their flaws."

Finally, after almost three years, I've found something close to forgiveness, even if I may never truly forgive myself. In this moment, I want nothing more than to kiss her, to grab onto her tight and never let her go. But instead, I stare at her, glowing in the effects of her newfound beauty in life—in herself.

I never stopped loving her, but I don't know how to tell her this when I can't even tell her the truth: how my father threatened to revoke what little inheritance I had if I dropped out of business school and continued seeing Julia—the girl who'd inspired me to be "so stupid," as he'd put it. How my mum's relapse had knocked my confidence in people's ability to change. How I'd lost hope. I just stare at her with deep admiration. A philosophy degree and a psychiatrist for a brother, and I still couldn't infer that, even in mounds of debt, I would only be happy living my own dreams. She pointed reality out to me when I couldn't see it, and for that, I abandoned her. Yet, here she is, seizing the day. She doesn't need me, but I want her. I have to try. *Try everything.*

I pull my hand from my pocket and extend it to her own on the table, dropping the locket in her palm.

"I think this belongs to you," I say in almost a whisper.

Her eyes gloss over with tears of disbelief as she stares deeply at the necklace with a small smile, and then looks back up at me.

"You kept it?" she asks, moved by my gesture.

"Of course I did." I look at her. "You were my swan song," I whisper.

She leans in across the table so that her face is close to mine.

"Let's get out of here," she says quietly.

Cambridge, MA

·

Top Left Star = Max's Neighborhood
Middle Star = Julia's Neighborhood
Bottom Star = The Coffee Shop

Fish

DEAD POETS SOCIETY   N.H. Kleinbaum   HYPERION
The BELL JAR   SYLVIA PLATH
EMILY DICKINSON'S POEMS   As She Preserved Them   Miller   Belknap Harvard

Woodford Boxing Center

Bean

Chance
Baylor

Musical Production

When the day is done and the sun has set
And you're taking in your final breath
You can't find your heart there's no beat
in your chest
And it's never enough when you're trying
your best

When you're all out of hope and you're
chasing the dawn
And you've emptied your glass and you're
three sails gone
When you're feeling so weak and they
tell you "be strong"
~~Maybe it's time to sing~~ your swan song
          I Promise You I'll be
We've all done some things that don't
make us so proud
And we've all seen some things we
can't say out loud
Even if you can't feel your heartbeat
it's still there
Maybe you just need someone to
remind you where

And we all must fall, So let us first
fly
I will follow you until the day that I
die
And our lives are short, we only have
so long
    So I'm asking you to be my swan song

The Dead Poet

SAVE
the
DATE

to celebrate
the wedding of

JULIA & MAXWELL

JUNE 21ST

invitation to follow

Julien
Kaminski

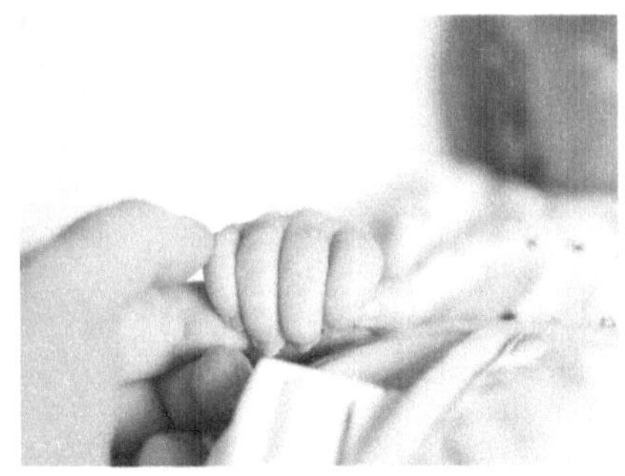

6
POUNDS
4 OUNCES

BORN
JULY 3RD

ACKNOWLEDGMENTS

Thank you to everyone who believed in me, and thank you to everyone who did not.

ABOUT THE AUTHOR

Isabel Bercaw is an author, entrepreneur, and soon to be Columbia University graduate (Class of 2025). Follow her on social media for more to her story and updates on upcoming events and signings.

Instagram: @isabel.bercaw
TikTok: @isabel.bercaw

SWAN SONG

www.ingramcontent.com/pod-product-compliance
Lightning Source LLC
Chambersburg PA
CBHW032238310726

48973CB00008B/2196